THE GRIM GRUESOME BOOKS

"just the thing for...readers...who want Dahl-style jokes and adventure." - *The Times*

"the sort of tale you can't stop reading even when it chills your blood." - *Primary Times*

"smashing...a real adventure story...horrible but also funny... A wonderful book" - *TES Connect*

"...the tales rattle along with great energy and fun... these books will be well loved by many children, who will wait impatiently for the next in the series." - *School Librarian*

"All the frosty bearded splendour of the Norse sagas condensed into a fun, thrilling tale for kids with a taste for high adventure...tipped to be a best-selling series." - *www.waterstones.com (5-star bookseller review)*

"full of twists and turns that you are desperate to follow." - *www.writeaway.org.uk*

"dramatic and vivid...fast-paced and enjoyable... plenty of humour throughout the story, too, which readers will love" - *Birmingham Post*

"brilliant, utterl~ ~ ~ ~ ~ I would rate this book 10/10...one of t   read." - *Joseph, 10, y~   Award*

GRIM GRUESOME
VIKING VILLAIN

in

THE RINGS OF DOOM

ROSALIND KERVEN

www.grimgruesome.com

First published in the UK by Talking Stone 2011

Text copyright © Rosalind Kerven 2011
Illustrations copyright © David Wyatt 2008, 2011

Talking Stone
an author-led publishing team
Swindonburn Cottage West, Sharperton,
Morpeth, Northumberland, NE65 7AP

ISBN: 978-0-9537454-6-3

For my editor Helen Greathead –
transformer of rough rocks into
gleaming Viking silver!

A big thank you also to:
artist David Wyatt,
designer Alison Gadsby,
and to
Dot Wilson and Stuart Manley
for their invaluable advice on horses
and games of strategy.

THE NORTH LANDS
A THOUSAND YEARS AGO
THE VIKING AGE

Come back through time to
the Viking realm of Iceland!

Imagine a land of savage beauty,
with no trees, no towns, no villages and no king.
Families lived well in the soft green valleys,
often travelling on horseback
between their scattered farms.
But beyond these lay a vast, untamed wilderness
of barren mountains, glaciers, hot rivers, deserts
and the lurking, dangerous menace of volcanic fire.

1

'Beware the Rings of Doom!'

'They're coming to get you!'

'Flee before it's too late!'

'Fear the Rings! Fear the evil one who brings them!'

Three weird-looking women in ragged, crow-black cloaks were trudging beside the rushing river in the peaceful summer grasslands of Salmon Valley. They whacked their walking sticks on the gravelly road, yelling at the tops of their voices:

'Hide – before they trap you!'

'Lock away your children! Beware the Rings of Doom!'

The first woman was as short as a dwarf and as fat as a pig. The second was as thin as a skeleton. The third was quite tall but bent almost double with an ugly hunchback. They all had wrinkly, wind-beaten faces, and their mouths were full of dark gaps where their teeth had fallen out.

They stopped in front of a small farmhouse nestling under the hills. Like all houses in Viking Iceland, it was made of turf – blocks of mud covered in thick grass, dotted with colourful flowers. It had a wooden chimney and a strong wooden door, but no windows.

'Anyone at home?' they all shouted together.

A boy with sandy-coloured hair came racing down the slope behind the house – and leaped right onto the roof.

'Flaming sheep poo!' he called down to them. 'Why are you making such a row?'

The short, fat woman wagged a plump, indignant finger at him. 'Mind your manners you cheeky brat!'

But the scraggy one said, 'Ah, you poor child! You don't realise! You are in terrible danger...'

'What danger?' the boy demanded.

The women all shook their heads and clamped their lips tightly shut.

'Get your mother, boy,' said the hunchbacked one. 'Ask her if we can sleep by your fireside tonight.'

'I can't,' said the boy. 'Ma's out.'

'Goddess Freyja's amber tears!' grumbled the short,

fat one. 'Every house we've called at this morning, there's been no farmwife at home. Where are we supposed to lay our poor old heads tonight?'

'Nowhere!' wailed the scraggy one.

'Out in the stony desert,' whined the hunchbacked one. 'Battered by the wind! Soaked by the rain!'

'Hold on. I'll get Sigrid,' muttered the boy. He jumped to the ground and disappeared into the house. A few moments later he came back, followed by a slightly older girl with the same sandy-coloured hair.

She looked at the women uncertainly. 'Our ma's up in the hills with the sheep and she won't be home until late,' she said. 'But I'm sure she won't mind if you come in.'

The weird women followed the children inside. In the entrance porch they hung up their cloaks, combed their greasy hair and smoothed down their tatty dresses and aprons. Then they all went through a second door into the main room.

A sunbeam was gleaming down the chimney and several oil lamps were flickering in stone holders, filling the room with soft light. The walls were all covered with plain wooden panelling. Protruding from them were wide, low benches covered in white and brown sheepskins. A fire piled with lumps of dried sheep dung was burning merrily in the centre of the beaten-mud floor.

Sigrid nipped through a small door into the storeroom, and came back carrying a wooden mug of frothy, sour milk for each of the women. They slurped their drinks, wiping their mouths with gnarled hands.

'Who are you?' said Magnus. 'Where are you from?'

'From nowhere,' said the hunchbacked woman gloomily.

'None of us has a home – nor a husband,' said the fat one. 'We haven't got *anything*: no silver, no sheep – no brats like you – nothing!'

The scraggy one screwed her wrinkled face into a miserable smile. 'We have got each other, of course,' she said. 'We're sisters, you see. I'm Helga.' She flung her arm round the short, fat one. 'This is Groa.' She grabbed the hunchbacked one's hand. 'And she's Vigdis.' She chuckled hoarsely. 'We've also got plenty of news and gossip.'

'And today our news comes with a grave warning,' said Vigdis. 'You see, my dears, we all suffer from nightmares. And they are full of dangerous omens.'

'Nightmares?' said Sigrid nervously. 'Omens?'

14

'Ya, child,' said Vigdis. Her voice was quavering. 'Every night we all dream of darkness. And gleaming within it, we see these mysterious Rings.'

'Circle within circle,' said Groa. 'Loop within loop.'

Sigrid shivered.

But Magnus said, 'When you say "Rings"…do you mean finger-rings? Arm-rings? Neck-rings?'

'What does it matter?' said Groa. 'Treasure of any kind always brings trouble: battles and wars, greed and envy.' She wobbled her double chins. 'Thieves and blood-guzzling pirates.'

Vigdis finished her milk and burped loudly. 'But *this* treasure, *these* Rings, will surely bring something even worse. We fear they will lead some innocent children to their doom.'

'*Children!*' cried Sigrid. 'Which children?'

'We can't tell you any more,' said Groa.

'Good,' said Sigrid. 'Because I don't want to hear any more. You're spooking me!'

'Huh!' sneered Magnus. 'Even a flea spooks you, Sigrid. Anyway, seeing as these ladies don't know what sort of rings they're talking about, they might not actually be *treasure*.'

The three hags all squirmed with surprise.

'What else could they be, boy?' snorted Helga.

'Well,' said Magnus knowingly. 'They might be something like...you know, rings of birds, flying in circles in the sky. Um...or the ring at the top of a volcano.'

'Thor's thunderbolts!' exclaimed Helga. 'We never thought of such possibilities. How clever you are!'

Magnus nodded smugly. 'I'm helpful too,' he said. 'I'll go and find our ma.'

'Show off!' Sigrid scowled at him. 'Goody goody!'

Magnus poked out his tongue at her. She thumped his arm. Magnus kicked her ankle, then scampered out.

'Tut-tut-tut,' said Helga.

'Children who fight never come to any good,' warned Vigdis.

'What disgraceful behaviour,' said Groa. 'You should both be ashamed.'

Sigrid turned bright red and her eyes filled with tears. She couldn't bring herself to look at the three women, so she picked up a piece of leather and an iron needle, and began sewing.

They sat watching her for a while. Then Helga said, more kindly, 'Are you making shoes, dear?'

Sigrid nodded and let out a big sigh. 'I'm *always* making shoes. Ma won't let me go out until I've made enough to last the whole family right through the summer. It's not fair!'

'You've got nothing to complain about,' said Vigdis severely. 'Look at *our* shoes.'

She lifted up one foot. Her bony toes were poking out through a large hole, and the whole shoe was falling to bits.

'We're desperate for some new ones,' said Groa. Her own shoes had rotted at the seams, revealing a podgy big toe with a jagged, grimy nail. 'We beg for shoes at every farm we visit, but folk always claim they haven't any to spare.'

Sigrid hesitated. 'I suppose I could give you some of ours,' she said reluctantly. 'But I'd have to ask Ma first – and Magnus is going to take ages fetching her, because he's so pathetic, he always has to *walk*.'

'And what's wrong with walking?' said Groa. 'We have to walk everywhere. We can't afford horses.'

'Well, Magnus could ride any horse on the farm – only he's too scared,' said Sigrid scornfully. 'So I end up having to take him around everywhere on the back of *my* horse. I'm fed up with it!'

She stitched away fiercely, biting her lip. Then suddenly she blurted out: 'I wish these Rings of Doom would get *him*!'

The three women all gasped loudly.

'Oh, oh, oh!' wailed Helga. 'What a shocking thing to say!'

'You wicked girl!' scolded Groa. Her double chins puffed out as if they would burst. 'Fancy wishing such evil on your own brother!'

'We can't stay in a house so full of hatred,' said Vigdis. 'Come on, sisters. There's still enough time to walk further down the valley and find a *decent* family to put us up tonight.'

They all got up and stomped out to the porch. Sigrid ran after them.

'You don't understand how nasty Magnus is,' she cried as they put on their cloaks. 'He's a pest – always getting me into trouble and...'

'Don't listen to her,' said Vigdis sharply.

Groa and Helga covered their ears with their hands and pulled up their hoods.

'It's Magnus's fault, not mine,' said Sigrid desperately. 'Please don't think badly of me. At least let me... Here.'

She slipped back into the main room, brought out three pairs of newly stitched shoes and thrust them at the women. 'You can have these,' she said.

Groa, Helga and Vigdis snatched them greedily. Then, snorting and harumphing, they waddled out of the door, and down the slope to the road.

2

Ma came riding back from the mountains all hot and bothered, with Magnus behind her on the horse. She was absolutely furious when Sigrid told her that the three women had already left.

'What a waste of my time, rushing back!' she fumed. 'You silly girl, Sigrid. Fancy sending poor Magnus all that way for nothing!'

'I didn't send him, Ma,' protested Sigrid. 'It was his own idea.'

Ma wasn't listening. She was too busy frowning at Magnus's filthy clothes and face. 'And look what a mess he's got himself into. Take him for a bath, will you, Sigrid. I promised Pa I'd go straight back.'

Sigrid sighed and went to saddle her horse, Faithful. He was a proud and handsome animal. His coat was rich grey, like the sky before a rainstorm. His thick tail hung almost to the ground, and his gentle eyes were fringed by a very long, well-combed mane.

Magnus clambered clumsily up behind her. Then they cantered up the Salmon Valley road to an area of rough ground. Here they both dismounted, left Faithful to graze beside some other horses and ran across the stony scrub towards a curious, low cloud of wispy steam. A murmur of invisible voices came drifting from it.

The steam was hanging over a waist-deep pool of water in the middle of some rocks. This water was *hot*. It bubbled up from a spring under the ground, and gave off a strong, sickly smell just like bad eggs. Despite this, it was completely pure and clear.

The voices belonged to three other children who were already sitting in the hot pool. Sigrid was really pleased to see that one of them was her good friend Asny. She was enjoying a luxurious soak alongside her two brothers: Kari who was the same age as Magnus; and Ref who was a couple of years older than the girls.

Sigrid and Magnus quickly undressed and slipped into the warm water beside them. Asny offered them a ball of fat-and-ashes soap, dotted with wild-flower petals. Magnus turned up his nose disdainfully, but

Sigrid used it to lather herself and wash her long hair. Then she lay back in the warm water and told the other three children about the three weird women and their disturbing warning.

'Of course,' Magnus interrupted her, 'the Rings of Doom probably aren't *treasure*. They're more likely to be…'

Sigrid rolled her eyes at Asny. 'Stop talking twaddle, Magnus.'

Magnus threw her a dirty look and nudged Kari. The two younger boys started jumping up and down beside Sigrid, splashing hot water into her face.

'Stop it!' she screamed. 'What in Thor's name are you doing? Stop, STOP!'

For the splashes were becoming more and more violent – even though the boys had stopped jumping up and down. She tried to get up. But the sloshing water kept throwing her off balance.

Then Asny started to moan: 'O-oohh. Aaw. I feel all dizzy…'

Something extraordinary was happening. The hot pool itself seemed to be lurching about, water splashing right over the rim. It was as if a giant was shaking it from side to side.

'This isn't our fault,' protested Kari.

KKKRAGHHAHRRGH! KKKRAGHHAHRRGH!

His words were drowned by a series of thunderous blasts that came rolling at them from somewhere beyond the far side of the river. The next moment, the sun disappeared. The air grew murky and dim.

'Yuck! What a stink!' groaned Asny. 'Now I feel sick too.'

The bad eggs smell hanging over the pool had grown so strong, it was like sitting in a liquid dung heap. Dry, warm dust coated their lips. They could scarcely breathe.

'Get out the water!' yelled Ref.

Frantically, clumsily, coughing and spluttering, they all hauled themselves onto the rocks.

The quivering ground slowly stilled. They stood up unsteadily.

'Whoo!' cried Magnus. 'Look at *that!*' He pointed across the wide river valley.

Pale against the eerie darkness, a gigantic plume of smoke was swelling over the peaks of some distant, snow-capped mountains.

The blasts grew even louder. An uneven line of brilliant yellow flames suddenly burst into the sky, shrouded in red smoke.

'Freyja's tears! It's just like it says in that poem about the gods,' breathed Sigrid. 'It must be Ragnarok – the end of the world! *Wolves will swallow the sun... The earth will tremble...*'

Magnus began to giggle. 'Don't be stupid. This isn't Ragnarok, you numbskull. It's an erupting volcano!'

3

'Quickly!' cried Ref. 'Get away!'

Still dripping wet, the five children pulled on their clothes. Coughing and stumbling, knees trembling, they raced across the rocks and scrub to the horses.

The air was filthy, the summer's day turned dark as a winter twilight. Above the distant mountains, flames zigzagged into the sky – red, orange, yellow and blinding white.

Magnus was babbling excitedly over the crackling and rumbling: 'At last – a real volcanic eruption! I've so longed to see one! You never believe me, Sigrid, but I'm always right. This is what the weird women dreamed about. The Doom is *fire* – pouring out of the Rings – the *holes* at the top of the volcano!'

Kari slapped him on the back. 'You're brilliant, Magnus!'

'Now I'll tell you something else,' said Magnus. 'That fire's going to melt all the snow on top of those mountains. Then it'll rush into the river and make terrible floods.'

'How can you know that?' said Sigrid sceptically.

'Because I listen to the men talking, that's how,' said Magnus. 'It's happened before in other places... And look, fish-head, I'm right again: the snow-melt's already on its way.'

He pointed across the river. The far side was all desert: a dry wilderness of rock and stone. However, a mass of streams had suddenly appeared in it, snaking from the distant mountains, glimmering in the glow of volcanic fire. As the children watched, the streams gradually gathered speed, merged into a single rapid gush of water – and came hurtling towards the river.

'If it floods over this side, we'll drown!' shrieked Kari.

'Get up the hill!' yelled Ref.

They jumped onto the horses and raced up the nearest slope. Once they reached a safe height, they stopped breathlessly to gaze back through the gloom.

'Phew!' breathed Asny. 'Look, the snow-melt's skirting round that big ridge on the far bank. It can't hit the river until further downstream. So this stretch of road shouldn't get flooded, and nor will our farms.'

'Let's ride further downstream to get a better view,' begged Magnus. 'Please, please, please! We'll be safe if we stay on high ground. I've got to see everything that happens.'

The three older children exchanged glances.

'Don't be crazy,' said Sigrid. 'We can hardly see where we're going, and this dust is suffocating. We should go straight home.'

'But then I'll miss everything,' whined Magnus. 'You always ruin things, Sigrid. Ref, you're the oldest. Tell her we've got to watch.'

'Well...I'd quite like to see what happens too,' said Ref. 'But it's dangerous, Magnus. As soon as I say, we're going straight back.'

Magnus nodded. Sigrid spluttered and swore under her breath. But then she had to calm Faithful, who had come over all nervous, stamping and tossing his head. And by the time she had finished, Ref, Asny and Kari were clambering into their saddles to ride on. Sigrid had no choice but to go with them, Magnus clinging behind her as usual.

The sure-footed horses carried the children along

the valley, following a sheep track that skirted the lower slopes of the hillside. They peered down through the twilight.

'Whee! Here it comes!' yelled Magnus.

The melt-water was hurtling past the ridge that Asny had spotted. It was a filthy, black, seething torrent, littered with tumbled rocks, topped by frothing scum. It poured into the river, surging over the banks, swirling across the shingle on either side.

'Hey, what's that?' yelled Kari. 'Can you hear it?'

Above the roar of water and the rumbling, crackling volcano, now there was a completely new sound, a curious, jingly, metallic rattling:

Kringle, kringle! Kringle, kringle!

Almost at once, it was followed by an anguished animal scream.

4

'It's over there!' cried Ref.

He pointed at the river. An enormous horse was standing chest-deep in the middle of it, a short way upstream from the seething vortex where the snow-melt came pouring in. The horse was black with a white mane that gleamed through the weird twilight as if threaded with silver. *NEHH!* it screamed. And as it struggled against the current and tossed its head, they heard again that curious rattling noise:

Kringle, kringle!

'Where on earth has it come from?' said Asny. 'Surely it hasn't waded out from the desert?'

'Look at the size of it,' said Ref. 'It's like a monster. Any normal horse would have gone under straightaway in a river that high, but it's still managing to stand upright.'

'It'll be swept away any moment,' said Magnus knowingly.

'Oh, poor thing!' cried Sigrid.

'No it won't,' said Asny firmly. 'We'll save it.' She fiddled with the side of her saddle. 'I've got some rope fixed on here – just the thing to pull the horse out.'

'*Girls* can't throw ropes,' sneered Magnus.

'We can!' snapped Sigrid.

Asny frantically tied a slip knot, looping the rope into a lasso.

They all rode carefully down the slope to the shingle, dismounted and crunched over the pebbles to the water's edge. Asny and Sigrid led the way, glancing nervously at the flood ahead, going as close as they dared to the stranded horse.

Kringle, kringle!

'Aha! So that's what the noise is,' said Sigrid, peering through the gloom. 'Can you see the rattle hanging from its bridle? That must be to stop it getting lost.'

'But it *is* lost, stupid,' said Magnus.

'I wonder what's happened to its owner?' said Kari.

'Never mind! Let's just rescue the poor thing,' said Sigrid. 'We can worry about who it belongs to later.'

She coughed and gagged. 'Aw, I can't stand this stink!'

KKKRAGHHAHRRGH!   KKKRAGHHAHRRGH!
The volcano rumbled on and on.

Asny tossed the lasso. It sped strongly through the murky air... But fell far short, flopping uselessly into the river.

'Missed,' said Magnus unnecessarily.

'Let me help,' said Sigrid.

The two girls scrambled precariously close to the water's edge and together dragged back the sopping lasso. Sharing the weight now, they hurled it out a second time.

'Missed aga…' Magnus began to scoff, then quickly swallowed his words.

This time the loop fell spot on over the horse's head. Asny twitched and jerked it, slipping it right down the horse's neck. The two girls exchanged smug grins and hauled on the rope together. Ref and Kari rushed over to help. The slip knot tightened, holding the horse firmly. The four children heaved with all their might.

Magnus ran up and down behind them, yelling imperiously: 'Heave-ho, you weaklings! Pull harder... *Harder,* I said!'

Even as they gradually hauled the horse in, the

current was trying to drag it towards the seething maelstrom. The children were forced to run beside it along the shingle. Soon they were barely twelve paces from the tumultuously cascading snow-melt. The floods slurped against the flow, seething over their feet. They all shrieked but kept on pulling. In the distance, smoke and flames billowed dazzlingly against the murky sky.

Slowly, slowly, the magnificent creature staggered towards them.

'Mind you don't topple the beast over,' shouted Magnus. 'Whoa! Don't let go!'

Sigrid loosened one hand from the rope to slap him, but he darted out of reach.

Now, even in the uncanny twilight, the horse was near enough for them to see every hair in its beautiful, silvery mane. It thrashed about, stirring up great spatters of spray, drenching their clothes. Step by slow step, the children inched backwards up the bank... And at last, the horse emerged from the river, violently shaking its head:

Kringle, kringle, kringle!

It was a full-grown male, a magnificent stallion. He towered over them, slim, long legged and muscular, twice as tall as any other horse they had ever seen. Water droplets shimmered in his silvery tail and mane.

KKKRAGHHAHRRGH! KKKRAGHHAHRRGH!

It sounded as if the earth was spewing out its guts. The ground was quaking again, the air thick with foul-smelling smut.

'I can hardly breathe,' groaned Kari. 'I feel like I'm going to puke.'

Sigrid coaxed the stallion over the shingle towards Faithful and the other horses. They were already pacing uneasily up and down, but the stallion seemed to spook them even more. He stood very still, watching them all. The rattle dangled from a strap of his bridle, a jumble of glimmering metal circles. Slowly he turned his inscrutable gaze from the horses to the children.

'Isn't he handsome!' said Ref. 'He's black as lava. And so shiny. And look at all that silver inlaid in his rattle.'

'Fit for a king!' said Magnus. 'I think I should be in charge of him.'

'You?' snorted Sigrid. 'When riding even a tiny horse scares the pants off your skinny little bottom? I'm surprised you're brave enough to look at this great big thing!'

Magnus made to thump her, but instead collapsed into a spluttery fit of coughing.

'We need to get away, fast,' said Ref firmly. 'Do you think the horse will follow us?'

Sigrid nodded. 'Hopefully. Come on, Magnus, stop showing off and get up behind me.'

Magnus opened his mouth to argue. But he hadn't brought his cloak, and a wind was whipping the volcanic dust into choking flurries. Grumbling, still coughing, he clambered up behind his sister.

They set off up the valley at a brisk pace, constantly glancing behind. Almost at once, the stallion began to trail after them:

Kringle, kringle!

'What a din!' moaned Kari. 'Can't we take that stupid rattle off him?'

'Better not,' said Ref. 'He must belong to someone important. If we damaged the rattle we might get into big trouble.'

5

Soon they reached Underhill Farm, where Sigrid and Magnus lived.

'Do you want to take the big horse home with you?' Sigrid called to the others.

'Of course they don't,' said Magnus quickly. 'We'll look after him.' He leaned forward and pinched Sigrid's arm. 'He's obviously valuable, you numbskull,' he hissed. 'If he's on our farm when his owner turns up, *we'll* get the reward.'

'I heard that, Magnus, you greedy maggot!' laughed Kari.

'You're the best with horses, Sigrid, you keep him,' said Asny quickly. 'To be honest, he gives me the creeps.'

Ref nodded. 'Me too. And the noise of the rattle is driving me mad.'

So the other three children rode on through the twilight to their own farm, leaving the mysterious stallion in the care of Sigrid and Magnus.

The volcano was still rumbling and crackling in the distance, but everything at Underhill Farm was eerily quiet.

'Ma, Pa!' the children shouted.

But nobody came, not even the housemaid. When they looked inside, the fire had gone out and there were no lights burning.

'They must still be up in the hills with the sheep,' said Sigrid wretchedly. 'Oh no! Supposing something dreadful's happened to them all, or they can't find their way back through this darkness? Please, mighty Thor, bring them home safely! And I was going to ask Ma what to do with this strange horse.'

Magnus folded his arms cockily. 'It's obvious what to do with him,' he said. 'You need to shut him in the stable. You can see he's a foreign breed – probably from some exotic country in the far south, where it's always really warm. He's been half-frozen in the river, and the volcano's scared him out of his mind. He needs quietness, warmth and the best hay.'

Sigrid pointed to the stable. 'Since you obviously

know more about horses than I do, Too-Scared-To-Ride Magnus,' she said sarcastically, '*you* take him there.'

Magnus didn't move.

Sigrid sighed. She let Faithful into the paddock with the other farm horses, then ran to open the stable door. As soon as she beckoned, the mysterious stallion stepped after her into the turf-walled building.

It was a relief to be indoors, away from the filth and noise of the eruption. At this time of year the stable wasn't normally used, and it smelled deliciously of clean, sweet straw. She felt along the shelf for a strike-a-light and an oil lamp, and soon the little building was softly lit by a dancing flame.

Sigrid fetched a brush. The stallion stood very still, allowing her to groom him as if he were doing her a great honour. When she was finished, he shook his head, making the rattle jingle. Sigrid covered him with a blanket and gave him a pile of hay.

The stallion stared at her. His gaze was unnerving, making her think of trolls and dark-elves. A chill ran through her. She hurried out and shut the door firmly behind her.

6

Sigrid and Magnus were both so exhausted that they put themselves to bed without any more arguments. They woke in the morning to find Ma and Pa safely home, having left the servants to guard the sheep at their hut in the hills.

Smoke was still pouring from the volcano. It was darker than ever, like perpetual night, lit by jagged dazzles of yellow and red flames leaping into the sky. Everywhere stank of bad eggs.

Before going outside, they all tied damp linen cloths round their faces to keep out the filth. Even so, they ended up spluttering and coughing. Pa dashed around the farm, sealing up the storage sheds to save their food supplies from spoiling. There was no noise from the stable, but in the paddock Faithful and the other horses paced miserably up and down, heads drooping. They were all coated with a thick layer of volcanic ash. The cows refused to be milked, and all had bad diarrhoea.

The family gathered around their fire for the morning meal, which tasted of bad eggs and cinders. They had scarcely finished eating when there was an urgent knocking at the door.

BAMM! BAMM! BAMM!

'Whoever can that be?' said Ma.

Pa stood up, pulled the damp cloth back over his nose and mouth and went to open it. Sigrid was curious to see who it was, so she sidled into the porch behind him. Magnus came too, elbowing her aside.

A very tall man with massive shoulders like a bull was standing outside. He was wrapped in a thick cloak, trimmed with fine black fur. This was fastened at the shoulder by an enormous silver brooch shaped like a distorted horse's head. His hood was pulled right forward. Underneath it, he too was protected from the volcanic dust with a cloth wrapped round his face.

'What do you call this farm? Who's in charge here?' he said. His voice, muffled by the cloth, was very deep and sonorous, like two lumps of iron clanging together. He pronounced each word with the precise manner of someone rather clever and important.

Pa sniffed. 'This is Underhill Farm,' he said. 'I'm the farmer here. Olaf, they call me. Who are you? And why ever are you travelling on such a dreadful day?'

The man held out an enormous hand, clad in a thick leather mitten.

'I'm from the West Fjords,' he answered. 'Chieftain Lygari.'

The two men shook hands.

'The West Fjords?' said Pa. 'That's at least twenty days' ride away, isn't it? What brings you to Salmon Valley?'

'I came to meet a horse dealer who lives in these parts,' said the chieftain. 'I've just sold him my old horse, and in return bought a much better and faster one. It's a splendid animal – a foreign breed.'

The two children pricked up their ears.

The chieftain went on: 'But unfortunately, when the volcano started erupting, it had a crazy fit – threw me off, then bolted into the desert. I've been searching right through the night, but there's no sign of it. *HAH*!'

He gave a roar of anger, making Magnus and Sigrid almost jump out of their skins.

'So I reckon that someone has found my horse and kept it for themselves,' he went on. '*Stolen* it.'

Pa shook his head. 'I can assure you, Chieftain, we've not seen any strange horses around here, neither straying nor stolen. Take a good look round our fields if you want. You'll only find our own ordinary farm horses.'

'Hmm,' said Chieftain Lygari. 'You must know that saying of Odin All-Father: *The more friendly a man's words, the more he has to hide.* I don't believe you, Farmer Olaf.'

There was an ominous silence.

'What did you say?' growled Pa.

'You heard me,' said Chieftain Lygari. 'I reckon you've stolen my horse. You've got him hidden somewhere.'

Pa made a half-hearted attempt to shoo the children back into the main room. Then he turned to a hook on the wall where a scabbard was hanging, and pulled out a rusty sword.

Sigrid clutched Magnus in alarm.

Pa pointed the sword at the chieftain. 'How dare you make false accusations against me!' he said.

Chieftain Lygari snorted behind his face-cloth. He

pulled off his mittens, revealing huge, hairy, battle-scarred hands. There was an ugly, scab-crusted stump where one of his little fingers should have been. He reached into the folds of his cloak and pulled out his own sword, which was almost twice as big as Pa's. He struck it through the air, then – *CLANG!* – smashed it down hard. Pa's sword vibrated wildly, then dropped from his hand to the floor.

Pa turned purple and held up his fists.

'I wouldn't pick a fight with me, if I were you,' said the chieftain quietly. 'I'm a very powerful man. At the Great Thing every year, I always stand right next to the Law Speaker.'

Pa looked uncertain. The Law Speaker was the most important man in Iceland. He was in charge at the Great Thing – the annual open-air public meeting when chieftains considered complaints against wrongdoers and decided how to punish them.

'I'm warning you,' said Chieftain Lygari. 'If I find my horse hidden here, your whole family will be in trouble.'

Sigrid pulled Magnus back into the main room. 'Thor's thunderbolts!' she hissed. 'What are we going to do? If only Pa hadn't been so busy this morning, we'd have been able to tell him about that horse.'

'It's your fault,' said Magnus. 'You wanted to rescue him.'

'But *you* insisted we should bring him here,' retorted Sigrid.

Magnus thought for a moment. 'Don't worry,' he said coolly. 'I'll deal with this.'

Before Sigrid could stop him, he stepped forward to stand beside Pa.

'Excuse me, Chieftain Lygari,' he said in a loud voice.

Magnus was exceptionally short for his age, and Chieftain Lygari was exceedingly tall. He loomed over Magnus like a giant. Magnus gazed steadily up at his masked, hooded face.

'I think your horse is in our stable, sir,' he said.

'WHAT?' roared Lygari. 'So I'm right. This farm is a den of thieves!'

Pa turned to his children in disbelief.

7

'My sister put him there,' Magnus blurted. 'Sigrid's really clever with horses. She can make them do anything.'

Sigrid blushed bright red.

'I saw her shoo a very big, strange horse into the stable and shut the door on it,' said Magnus.

Pa's mouth dropped open. 'I haven't a clue what this is about,' he told the chieftain. 'I was up in the mountains until late last night, and so was my wife. The children were already asleep by the time we got home and they never mentioned any horse this morning.'

He grabbed Sigrid by the shoulders. 'Why didn't you tell me about this?'

'I haven't had a chance, Pa,' protested Sigrid, twisting her hands together. 'Anyway, Magnus was involved too. We didn't *steal* the horse, Chieftain Lygari sir. I swear on mighty Thor – on Odin – that we didn't! We *rescued* him. He was almost drowning in the flood from the volcano, and we pulled him out, with our friends. We saved his life!'

'Where is he?' the chieftain growled.

Pa looked very embarrassed. 'You'd better show him, Sigrid,' he said tightly.

Sigrid grimaced at Magnus. Then she led the chieftain across the grass to the stable and pushed open the door.

In the gloom, the great black stallion stood by the far wall, still as a rune-stone. But as soon as the choking volcanic dust blew into the building, he began tossing his head. The rattle jangled gratingly.

The chieftain stooped and stepped inside.

'He's still acting like he's been spooked,' he said. 'He's no use to me like this: he'll only bolt again. Odin's pus-leaking eye-socket!' He whacked his sword angrily against the stable wall. 'That horse dealer's sold me a dud. I'll slice off his head when I find him again!'

'Calm the horse down, can't you, Sigrid?' Pa called.

Sigrid slipped past Chieftain Lygari and went up to

the stallion. 'There, my beauty,' she said. She tried to make her voice soothing, even though she could scarcely keep it steady. She was drenched in cold sweat. She held out her hand to the horse, letting him sniff her. She reached up to his smooth, elegant neck and gently stroked him.

'You're all right,' she whispered. 'There, there, your new master's here. He's going to take you right away from this horrid volcano. Everything's fine now. Come on.'

Her voice and her touch were like magic: almost at once, the stallion relaxed. Sigrid grasped his bridle, fixed a lead-rope to it and led him slowly out of the stable. He didn't resist. *Kringle, kringle!* went the rattle.

Because Sigrid was walking backwards, she almost toppled into the chieftain. At once she was hit by a foul and pungent smell, like rotten meat, even stronger than the volcanic stench. She retched.

'Excuse me!' she mumbled, stepping quickly out of his way.

Chieftain Lygari snatched the lead-rope from her. He ran his great, hairy, nine-fingered hands over the horse's body. He lifted up the horse's eyelids to examine his eyes. He pulled back the horse's lips to check his teeth. Finally, he put the sword away and cleared his throat loudly.

'Luckily, he doesn't seem to have come to any harm,' he said gruffly. 'Apologies for my false accusation, Farmer Olaf. You should be proud of your daughter. She's both helpful and very capable.'

Pa looked relieved. 'Apology accepted,' he grunted.

The chieftain snapped his fingers at Sigrid. 'You saved my horse, so I must give you a reward, girl. As Odin All-Father said: *Mutual giving makes for friendship*. What would you like?'

Magnus came up right next to Sigrid and hissed under his breath. 'I told you it was valuable! Ask for a load of treasure.'

'That's very good of you, Lygari,' said Pa. 'I'm sure she'd be happy with something small and pretty, like a finger-ring.'

'No, Pa, not a ring,' she cried. 'They're dangerous!'

Pa raised his eyebrows in surprise.

'Well, I've never heard of a girl who doesn't like rings before!' exclaimed the Chieftain. 'But never mind, Sigrid, I know a much better reward for someone with your talents. You shall have a new horse of your own, in return for saving mine.'

'That's far too much for such a small deed,' said Pa. 'Anyway, my wife breeds good horses here on the farm.'

'I don't want a new horse,' said Sigrid. 'I've got my Faithful.'

The chieftain ignored her. 'Now listen, Farmer Olaf,' he said. 'I'll come back some time after Yule Feast, with a horse for your daughter that's far better than anything your wife has ever bred.' He slapped the black stallion's flank. 'Ya, it'll be almost as good as this one.'

8

'Pa said it was all thanks to me that the chieftain apologised, and that they didn't end up having a big fight,' said Sigrid proudly. 'Even Ma said I did well to calm the chieftain's horse so quickly. That's the first time ever that they've both praised *me*, instead of stupid, poo-faced Magnus.'

'Well done,' said Asny.

The air outside was still full of dust, so the two girls were sitting in the storeroom at River Bend Farm, where Asny lived.

'But then Ma went and spoiled it,' said Sigrid crossly. 'I was just pointing out to Magnus how *I* was the one who saved the situation, not him – and she overheard. She lashed out at me for showing off.'

Asny clucked sympathetically.

'And then it was the usual story,' Sigrid went on.

49

'You know, twisting everything round so that Magnus gets the best of it. Ma said that when Chieftain Lygari comes back next year, she'll make sure Magnus gets a chance to talk to him properly…' She put on a silly voice: '…So that he can "see what a clever young man he is". Huh! All they want is for Magnus to do well. They don't care about me.'

'I'm sure they do, but in a different way,' said Asny.

'They don't!' Sigrid insisted. 'Chieftain Lygari's coming back with a reward for *me*, not Magnus. But I bet, once he's given me this stupid horse – that I don't even want – I'll be pushed out of the way. You get on with your brothers, so you can't imagine how awful it is, being stuck with pesky Magnus. He's like a permanent flea bite, irritating me all day long. I wish, I WISH I could get rid of him!'

9

The volcanic eruption went on all through the summer. It spewed endless clouds of ash into the air – mostly fine and powdery, but sometimes falling in small, glassy shards like a hailstorm.

At Underhill Farm, the house door was kept tightly shut, but that didn't stop ash falling down the chimney and seeping through the cracks. Ma, Sigrid and the housemaid swept, dusted and shook out the bedding all day long, but everything still seemed grubby. The food tasted burned and gritty. They still had to wear cloths over their faces whenever they went outside.

The grass had disappeared under a thick layer of ash. Pa's farmhands took the sheep and cattle to the furthest hills, away from the worst of it. But the horses were needed at the farm, even though there wasn't enough for them to eat. Poor Faithful became quite skinny.

Late one evening a messenger – wearing the usual face-cloth – came galloping up Salmon Valley from the north coast and knocked at the door.

'What's up?' said Pa. Sigrid and Magnus peered out nosily behind him.

'Odin's eye socket! I'm glad I've found you at last,' grumbled the messenger. 'I can't wait to get out of this filthy valley. I've got news for you, Farmer Olaf – both bad and good. Here's the bad stuff first: your Uncle Eyvind has just died.'

Pa stared at him. 'Who's Uncle Eyvind?'

'I've come a long way, so don't play the fool with me,' snapped the messenger.

'Sorry,' said Pa, 'but I've never heard of him. Are you sure you're not looking for someone else?'

'Sure as sure,' said the messenger. 'Eyvind was your father's brother's wife's cousin's mother's brother-in-law.'

'Say that again?' said Pa.

'Mind you, it's not surprising you don't remember him, because apparently there was some big bust-up between the various branches of the families, when you were still a boy. Anyway, he's dead now. And his other relations have ordered me to deliver this.'

He handed Pa a flat piece of wood, carved with rows of spiky lines.

'Can you read runes?' he said.

'I can!' cried Magnus. Pa let him take the wood. Magnus studied the spiky rune-letters, then read them out in a clear, confident voice:

ᛏᚠᛁᛏᛏ : ᚤᛏᛏ : ᚦᛏᚺ : ᚱᛚᛏᚺ

'EYVIND MADE THESE RUNES

ᚱᛏᛏ : ᚦᛏᚤ : ᚠᛏᛏ : ᛁ : ᛏᛁ

READ THEM WHEN I DIE.

ᛁ : ᚷᛁᛏ : ᛏᚱᛁᚺᛤ : ᛚᛏᛏᛤ : ᚤᛁ : ᚱᛚᛒᛁᚺᚵ : ᛏᛚᚤᛒ

I HID TREASURE UNDER MY RUBBISH DUMP

ᚠᛁᚠ : ᛁᛏ : ᛏᛚ : ᚺᛁᚤᚱᛁᛏ : ᚠᛏᚤᚠᚺᛏᚠᛏ

GIVE IT TO SIGRID OLAF'S-DAUGHTER

ᛏᛚ : ᚤᚤᚠ : ᛒᛁᚺ : ᛒᛏᛏᚠᛁᛏ : ᚠᛤ : ᚠᛏᚤᛁᚠᛁᚺ

TO MAKE PEACE BETWEEN OUR FAMILIES'

'Dwarf spit, Sigrid!' said Pa. 'You've come into an inheritance. You lucky girl!'

Sigrid let out a long breath. Her eyes were shining.

'What about me?' said Magnus indignantly, handing back the rune-stone. 'Don't I get anything?'

The messenger ignored him. He threw back his cloak. Tied to his belt, they saw a small bundle wrapped in white linen. He unfastened it and thrust it at Sigrid.

'Here you are, girl, take it,' he said. 'Right, I'm getting out of this filthy place.' And before they could ask him any more, he galloped off.

They all trooped back inside. Ma was as astonished as Pa to hear about the unknown uncle and Sigrid's surprise inheritance.

'Let's see it then,' she said.

Sigrid laid the bundle carefully on the high-seat and unwrapped the linen. Inside were five beautifully worked pieces of jewellery: a delicate neck-ring made of twisted silver strands, two silver arm-rings stamped with exquisite patterns and two matching finger-rings.

'Oh, rings…' she said uncertainly.

'Freyja's tears!' exclaimed Ma. 'What a generous inheritance, especially considering none of us even knew this Uncle Eyvind.'

'You'll be the grandest girl in the valley, wearing those,' said Pa.

But Magnus leaped forward, spreading his arms between Sigrid and the treasure.

'Keep away!' he yelled. 'Don't touch them! Remember the warning from those weird women!'

'You mean those mad blabbermouths that had me running back from the hills for nothing?' said Ma. 'What have they got to do with this?'

'If you'd met them, Ma, you'd have realised they weren't mad,' said Magnus. 'They told us very clearly to "Beware the Rings of Doom". It can't be a coincidence that just a few months later a mysterious stranger has given these rings to Sigrid, completely out of the blue. They *must* be the Rings of Doom. You know I'm right, Sigrid. When Chieftain Lygari was here, you said yourself that rings are dangerous.'

'But they're so beautiful,' said Sigrid wistfully. 'Anyway, Magnus, you claimed before that the Rings of Doom meant the volcano erupting. You didn't believe they were jewellery.'

'That was just an intelligent guess, because until now there weren't any *real* rings,' said Magnus.

'You make things up to suit yourself,' grumbled Sigrid. 'It's because you're jealous that – for once – I've got something and you haven't.'

'I'm concerned for your safety, Sigrid,' said Magnus airily. 'I don't want something awful happening if you wear these rings.'

Ma ruffled his hair doubtfully.

Pa said, 'Magnus is a very sensible lad. We should listen to him.'

The five rings gleamed in the lamplight. Sigrid gazed longingly at them. 'How can jewellery be dangerous? Like you said, Ma, those women were probably just crazy old gossips.'

She picked up one of the finger-rings and made to slip it on.

'Leave it!' screamed Magnus. 'It's spooked!'

Ma sighed loudly. 'Sigrid, it's a great shame, but... just in case Magnus is right, you'd better put it down.'

'The only time in my life that something good happens to me, you ruin it, Magnus,' cried Sigrid. 'I can't tell you how much I HATE YOU!'

She hurled the ring back onto the cloth.

'You don't deserve this gift anyway, you little madam,' said Ma sourly. 'I'm going to wrap the treasure up again and put it away. The volcano's caused us enough problems. We certainly don't want to take any risks and add to them!'

10

Although Magnus was embarrassingly small for his age and too scared to ride a horse, he was very ambitious. He had lots of plans for when he grew up. The main one was, somehow, to become a chieftain.

He knew this wouldn't be easy, because most chieftains had fathers or uncles who had been chieftains before them. However, he had told Pa about his ambition. Pa had got very excited, and promised to do everything he could to help him achieve it.

He taught Magnus all the stories he knew about the gods and heroes, and the history of Iceland and the other North Lands. He got a friend of his to show Magnus how to carve and read runes. When a travelling poet passed through Salmon Valley, Pa paid him to teach Magnus how poems were composed, with all their complex rules of imagery, rhythm and rhyme.

And whenever Pa got together with the other local farmers, he let Magnus listen to them talking. As a result, Magnus was much more knowledgeable than any of the other boys in Salmon Valley.

One afternoon, months after the volcano had finished erupting, Ma sent Magnus outside to fetch a bucket of water. This came from a spring – a hollow where fresh, cold water bubbled up naturally from the ground. On his way back, he heard the distant clatter of hooves. Then a hauntingly familiar sound drifted towards him on the wind:

Kringle, kringle!

It was late winter. The layer of ash had disappeared under a thick crust of frozen snow. A watery sun was shining, casting vivid, dark blue shadows. Amongst them, Magnus made out the silhouette of a horse and a rider in a billowing cloak moving slowly towards him.

I bet that's Chieftain Lygari, he thought.

Hastily he put the bucket down by the door, then dusted himself off and straightened his clothes. The chieftain turned up the track to Underhill Farm. He was leading a second horse behind him. Magnus hadn't noticed it at first, because it was pure white and thus almost invisible against the snow. It was short and stocky like any Icelandic farm horse, but its face was unusually delicate. Its mane and tail were the colour of clotted cream, neatly trimmed and expertly brushed. Like the chieftain's horse, it had a rattle dangling from its bridle.

Chieftain Lygari rode grandly up to the house and dismounted with a flourish. Magnus noticed that he still wore a protective face-cloth under his hood – even though the air was now completely clean.

'Good day, sir,' said Magnus politely. 'Welcome back.'

He shook hands with the chieftain in a very adult way, trying not to wince at Lygari's ugly battle scars and his bone-crushing grip. He tethered the two horses carefully and led the chieftain into the house.

Asny was visiting there too, helping Sigrid and Ma on the weaving loom. They all jumped up when they saw their distinguished guest.

'Greetings, good lady,' the chieftain said, shaking hands cheerfully with Ma. The hostility of his previous visit seemed completely forgotten: today he was overflowing with friendliness and warmth.

He turned to Sigrid. 'Ahah, there you are, my little horse expert.' He patted her heartily on the head. 'I've brought your reward, just as I promised. Come outside, my dear. Come and see.'

Sigrid blushed and got up nervously. The chieftain led her out into the icy yard, followed by Ma, Magnus and Asny.

'Oh, what a beauty!' cried Ma, admiring the white horse with an expert eye. 'You don't see many with that pure colour. She's beautifully groomed too. You've gone to such trouble, Chieftain Lygari, bringing her all the way here from the West Fjords – and in such wintry weather too! That's very good of you.'

Sigrid glanced across the paddock to Faithful. He stuck out his head towards her quizzically, ears pricked forward. He gave a worried, high-pitched *Ne-e-eh*! She blew him a kiss.

'You must stay with us tonight, sir,' said Ma to Chieftain Lygari. 'I'll cook a special meal.'

'Are you sure, good lady?' said the chieftain. 'Aren't you short of food since the volcanic eruption?'

'Not at all,' Ma assured him. 'A really rich crop of grass grew up through the ash, and the animals my husband slaughtered last autumn were the fattest we've ever known. We've still got a huge stock of meat.'

'Then I shall be delighted,' said the chieftain. He turned back to Sigrid. 'This horse is only part of the reward I promised you, my dear,' he said. 'I have a wonderful surprise planned for you as well.'

'What sort of surprise?' said Sigrid.

'Tut, tut,' said the chieftain. 'Wait and see. Meanwhile, come and get to know your new steed.'

He took her wrist in his enormous hand – Sigrid was glad it wasn't the one with the revolting stump – and placed her fingertips on the white horse's neck.

'She's called Elf,' he said. 'She's a very special horse.'

'Aren't you going to say thank you, Sigrid?' Ma scolded.

Sigrid patted Elf dutifully and mumbled an insincere 'thank you' to the chieftain. Across the pasture, she saw Faithful drop a big dollop of watery dung onto the snow, his ears flickering anxiously.

Magnus moved to a position where the chieftain would be able to see him. 'In what way is Elf special?' he asked.

'She is completely fearless and totally sure-footed,'

said Chieftain Lygari. 'She's almost a match for my own horse here, Haski. You can ride her anywhere and she won't let you down. Even the wildest, most lonely landscapes don't bother her, and the rougher the ground, the steadier she goes.'

'That sounds very impressive, sir,' said Magnus brightly.

'Indeed,' said Chieftain Lygari.

Sigrid elbowed Magnus aside. 'Why do both horses have those funny rattles on their bridles?' she asked.

'It's a training aid,' said Lygari. 'We chieftains always use them. Whatever you do, Sigrid, don't take Elf's rattle off, or she won't obey you.'

'That's interesting,' said Ma. 'I've been breeding and breaking in horses for years, but I've never heard of that method before. How does it work?'

Lygari gave a mysterious rumble of laughter and bent down so that his masked head was on a level with Sigrid's. 'Always remember that Elf is a gift from me,' he said gravely. 'Treat her with the care she deserves. Devote yourself to looking after her. As for that bedraggled old horse you used to ride: don't waste any more time on him.'

Sigrid looked across to Faithful again. She felt very

uncomfortable and didn't know what to say.

She felt something nudging her arm and turned to see the chieftain's horse, Haski, staring at her, nostrils flared. He drew back his head and nudged her again, forcing her to turn back to Elf.

Although Chieftain Lygari's eyes were invisible, she sensed that he was watching her.

She patted Elf's nose dutifully. Elf's coat was delightfully smooth, much softer than Faithful's. Her mane glimmered as if it were made of fine-spun foreign silk. She was certainly stunningly beautiful. Yet she stayed stock-still, head down, ears drooping, as if she couldn't feel – or didn't care – that Sigrid was touching her.

11

Some people claim that animals don't have feelings; but if you have a pet of your own, you will know that isn't true. From the moment Elf arrived at Underhill Farm, Faithful was overwhelmed with feelings. Most of them were not good.

He saw Sigrid looking at him critically. *WORRY.* He saw her patting Elf. *JEALOUSY.*

Nevertheless, he tried to make Elf welcome. While the humans were talking, Faithful went up close to her and gently scratched her back with his teeth in a very friendly way. At first Elf didn't respond at all, standing dead still as if she were lost in a deep sleep. When Faithful gently persisted, Elf roused herself to pull back her lips, half-heartedly threatening to bite.

Faithful didn't give up. He whinnied and shook his head at her, inviting her to walk across the paddock to join the other horses who were sharing some hay piled up on top of the snow. But Elf just narrowed her eyes and swished her creamy tail disdainfully.

The other farm horses ignored her.

12

Chieftain Lygari turned his attention to Magnus. 'Now young man,' he said in a low voice. 'I hope you're not going to be jealous of your sister. She's only a girl, and girls need presents to stop them whining. She's not destined to achieve great things – unlike you.'

Magnus threw a very smug look at Sigrid.

'Don't you two dare start fighting,' said Ma wearily. 'Sigrid, as Chieftain Lygari's horse is such an exotic breed, he needs to be put indoors straightaway in this cold weather. Take him to the stable – and Elf too, to help her settle in. Make sure they've got enough to eat.'

Sigrid muttered under her breath and led the two horses away.

Asny went to follow her, but Ma called out, 'Not you, Asny. It's getting dark. You'd better fetch your own horse and ride home before your mother starts to worry.'

She turned back to the chieftain. 'Do come into the house, Chieftain Lygari. You can have a drink and get warm while I prepare the meal.'

The chieftain unclipped a large, very battered leather bag from Haski's saddle, then crunched across the snow with it beside Ma. Magnus trailed behind.

'Chieftain,' said Ma thoughtfully. 'I've been wondering… With all your great wisdom and experience, please could you give me some advice?'

'Of course, good lady, I'd be delighted,' said Lygari.

So Ma told him about the weird women's warning of the Rings of Doom, and then about the strange set of rings that Sigrid had recently inherited from a mysterious relative.

The chieftain listened carefully. He pondered the problem silently as he followed Ma indoors, dumped his saddlebag in the porch and stamped the snow off his boots.

They sat down on either side of the fire and at last he said, 'Good lady, do you believe what the messenger told your husband? Why would someone you have never heard of leave your daughter such a marvellous treasure?'

Ma shook her head. 'That's just the thing. We've no idea.'

'It sounds very suspicious,' said the chieftain. 'Especially coming so soon after your children have been warned about these Rings of Doom.'

'Oh dear,' said Ma. 'That's just what we thought.'

The chieftain leaned forward confidingly, slapping his hands down on his great knees. His finger-stump quivered.

'I don't want to worry you unduly,' he went on. 'But I should tell you that just before the first snowfall, the Law Speaker sent a disturbing message round to all the chieftains in Iceland.' He lowered his voice. 'Have you heard of the evil child killer, Grim Gruesome?'

Ma went pale. 'Ya, of course I have. He's the most dangerous man in the North Lands! But he's never been seen in Iceland, has he?'

'I'm afraid he has,' said Lygari.

Magnus slid along the wall-bench, to be sure he could hear every word.

The chieftain said, 'While everyone was distracted by the volcanic eruption last year, he crossed the sea from the islands north of Britain, and landed here unnoticed. No doubt, the weird women that your children met heard rumours about this, causing both their bad dreams and their warning.'

'But what's Grim Gruesome got to do with the treasure left to Sigrid?' said Ma.

'It's most likely a trap,' said the chieftain gravely. 'I cannot tell you how he intends it to work, for the villain always acts in a very devious way. But the fact that the rings were left to a *child* should immediately put you on your guard. The messenger who brought them may well be in league with Grim Gruesome.'

'Oh dear!' cried Ma.

'I advise you not to let Sigrid wear these rings,' said Lygari. 'Don't take any risks.'

'She hasn't, luckily,' said Ma in a fluster. 'But what should we do with them?'

'Destroy them,' said Lygari crisply.

'But how?' cried Ma. 'And will that really keep the children safe from Grim Gruesome?'

The chieftain held out his finger-stump to the warmth of the fire. 'I can easily do this for you,' he said, 'Firstly, I can melt the rings down...'

'That sounds a very good idea,' said Ma.

'Then,' the chieftain went on, 'to ensure that even the melted silver can't cause any harm, I can carry out a short ceremony in the name of Odin, to cleanse it and remove any evil influences. If you wish to be rid of it completely, I could then take away the remains and bury them deep underground. That should certainly protect your children.'

Ma gave a little shudder. 'Thank you so much!' she said. 'That would be a great relief!'

13

Just as Sigrid's mother had told her to do, Asny started across the field to find her horse amongst the group of shaggy-maned animals munching on the hay bale. But instead of riding straight home, she hung around, watching Ma, Magnus and the chieftain go into the house. Once they were inside, she sneaked after them, crept into the porch and pressed her eye to a crack by the inner door, listening intently. Then she slipped out and ran across the snow to find Sigrid in the stable.

Sigrid had already covered Haski with a blanket and now she was busy seeing to Elf. Asny rushed inside and slammed the door behind her.

'Hey, open it,' called Sigrid, stumbling against a feeding trough. 'I can't see what I'm doing.'

Asny grabbed her arm. 'No, keep it shut,' she whispered. 'We don't want *him* to hear.'

'Who? Magnus?'

'No, stupid, the chieftain. He's *scary*, Sigrid.'

'Chieftains have to be scary,' said Sigrid indifferently. 'That's why people obey them.'

'Ya, but but other chieftains don't keep their faces hidden, like Lygari does,' said Asny. 'There hasn't been any volcanic ash in the air for months, so why is he still wearing a cloth over his face?'

'He comes from the other side of the country,' said Sigrid. 'So he probably didn't realise the air was clear until he got here. Anyway, I'll be able to tell you what he looks like tomorrow. I'll see when I go inside.'

'I bet you don't,' said Asny. 'I've just sneaked into your house to find out what was going on.'

'Thunderbolts!' cried Sigrid. 'You're so nosy.'

'The chieftain's sitting by your fire,' Asny went on. 'You know how warm your house always is? Well, despite that, he's still wearing his cloak, with the hood right up.'

'So what?' said Sigrid.

'It's as if he doesn't want anyone to see his face,' said Asny. 'And I could hear him talking. He was asking Magnus why you two don't get on – as if he was trying to stir things up between you. He gives me the creeps.'

In the dark, Haski shifted, making his rattle jangle softly. The white horse, Elf, stood absolutely still.

'Huh!' said Sigrid. 'Nobody can "stir things up" between me and my brother – because they're already as bad as they could possibly be. I can't tell you how much I *hate* him!'

'If only you would try harder to get on with him...' sighed Asny.

'You sound like my ma! Always blaming me – when it's *Magnus* who's the two-faced, self-centered, puffed-up piece of pig poo!' Sigrid spat the words out. 'He always gets the best of everything. All *I* ever get is tellings off. I wish, I wish, I WISH I could get rid of him!'

'That's really horrible!' cried Asny. 'How can you say such a wicked thing? Take it back, Sigrid, please! Or I'll...I'll…'

'You'll what?' said Sigrid coldly.

'I...I...I won't be your friend any more!' cried Asny.

'Huh! You obviously care about Magnus more than me,' said Sigrid. 'In that case, Asny, I don't *want* you as my friend!'

Asny gasped. Then, without another word, she stomped out into the frosty twilight.

14

Faithful's head was filled by a horrible memory of Sigrid patting Elf. She had done it not once but twice – as if they belonged together. That wasn't right. Sigrid was *his*.

He didn't eat any of the hay that the other horses were enjoying. He couldn't even concentrate on nibbling grass. He just stood very still, waiting for Sigrid to come and comfort him. While he waited, he couldn't help dribbling. He dropped a long stream of gooey dung onto the snow, much more than usual. Every so often, he made an anxious squeal, a long, high-pitched *'Ne-eh-ehh!'*

He saw Asny stomping out of the stable and riding away.

Still he waited patiently. The winter's twilight thickened into darkness.

He heard Sigrid's angry footsteps. She came back into the field and started calling all the farm horses into the stable for the night.

Faithful stayed where he was. Once all the other horses were inside, Sigrid came over and stroked him. But he could feel the tension in her fingers and she smelled all wrong – of Haski and Elf, alien and unearthly. Also, she smelled of a strange, bad emotion. He didn't understand what any of this meant.

Faithful nuzzled her earnestly. He made little nickering love-noises at her, then walked meekly into the stable behind her. But after Sigrid had left him, he felt as if he was sinking into a deep, dark bog of misery.

15

Sigrid was still screwed up with fury at Asny when she ran into the house. But she was quickly distracted by Chieftain Lygari. He was sitting next to Pa, between the polished wooden pillars of the high-seat, talking in a loud, rasping voice. His long legs were stretched out towards the fire, clad in thick, high, whale hide boots. Sure enough, he was still wearing his cloak with the hood up, even though the room was warm and cosy.

However, there was a perfectly normal explanation for this. For Ma called out to Sigrid, 'Shut the door tightly, please. The chieftain has a bad cold and he needs to keep out of the draught.'

Sigrid did as she was told, then sat down on the opposite bench next to her brother.

Magnus whispered, 'The cloth over his face is to stop him sneezing.'

A pot of Ma's best blood sausages was bubbling away over the fire. Sigrid's mouth watered.

Chieftain Lygari was in the middle of telling the family all about last year's meeting of the Great Thing. He was very entertaining, and kept making them exclaim and chuckle over juicy bits of gossip about the other chieftains and their wives. However, every so often he spoke of more serious matters. At this, Magnus nodded earnestly, and once or twice even interrupted to ask some questions.

'Show off!' Sigrid hissed at him.

'Shut up, you ignoramus!' Magnus hissed back.

To their great embarrassment, Chieftain Lygari turned his head in their direction. They both blushed and sat up straight.

'Stop arguing, children,' said the chieftain. 'Sigrid, you need to listen very carefully. Your mother has asked my advice about the mysterious silver rings that you inherited.'

'Oh!' cried Sigrid. 'Are they…?'

'I'm afraid they may be a dangerous trap,' said Chieftain Lygari.

'I was right,' cried Magnus excitedly. 'He reckons they *are* the Rings of Doom! He thinks the trap's been set by that villain Grim Gruesome! You know, the evil child killer – the one that you're always trying to scare me with…'

'Sigrid!' said Ma severely. 'You should be ashamed of yourself. Fancy frightening poor Magnus like that!'

Chieftain Lygari pinched the face-cloth over his nose and blew on it loudly, staining it with a splodge of wet, yellow snot.

Under cover of this noise, Sigrid muttered, 'There you go again, getting me into trouble, you brat.'

'Are you listening, Sigrid?' frowned Ma. 'Grim Gruesome isn't just a character in a story, you know. He's a real, live thug! And the chieftain says he's hiding in Iceland – possibly somewhere nearby!'

Chieftain Lygari cleared his throat gratingly and went on: 'Indeed, Sigrid. Grim Gruesome is probably lurking in the mountains across the river.' His voice was very solemn. 'I fear that he sent these mysterious rings to mark you both out as his next victims.'

Sigrid went very pale. 'Sorry, Ma,' she said in a small voice. 'Honestly, I had no idea that Grim Gruesome could really come anywhere near here.' She bit her lip and shivered. 'Oh, Chieftain Lygari, sir, please save us from him!'

She glanced at Magnus, about to apologise to him too...but quickly changed her mind when he poked out his tongue at her.

'Don't worry,' said the chieftain. 'I shall throw him right off your trail – by destroying the rings, cleansing the silver with a simple ritual, and then burying the remains.'

'You'd best get on with it straightaway,' said Pa.

Lygari nodded.

Pa fetched the linen package from a wooden chest. Chieftain Lygari placed it on the bench beside the high-seat and unwrapped it. The silver neck-ring, arm-rings and finger-rings gleamed in the firelight. He beckoned the children closer.

'To avoid their evil power, don't touch them at all,' he warned. 'However, you may look at them more closely and admire their splendid workmanship. What a pity you can't wear them, Sigrid my dear. They would have made you look magnificent.'

He shooed the children away.

'Let us begin,' he said. 'I need a cauldron, please, good lady.'

Ma brought a selection of cooking pots from the storeroom. The chieftain chose the deepest one. He unhooked the pot of sausages from the chain hanging over the fire, then put the new cauldron in its place. Carefully, he lowered the chain until the cauldron was resting right on top of the flames.

'Stoke up the fire,' he ordered.

Ma selected some big pats of dried sheep-dung from a stack in the corner and tossed them onto the fire. She jiggled the stones at one end of the fire-pit to let in more air, and whacked the dung with a poker. The flames sizzled, filling the room with smoke and heat. The chieftain took the poker from her and thrust it into the pot, pushing the rings around with it as if he were stirring food.

'They're melting,' cried Sigrid, peering inside. 'Oh, it's such a shame! They were so pretty.'

'The fire needs to be hotter still,' said the chieftain softly. 'Stand back, children

Pa fetched a set of wood-and-leather bellows and worked them open-and-shut, open-and-shut, until the fire flared right up. The room grew hotter and hotter. Everyone began to sweat and puff and roll up their sleeves – except the chieftain. With his cloak and hood wrapped tightly around him, he was still dressed for travelling in the snow.

They all waited.

Chieftain Lygari rocked the cauldron gently, muttering to himself. They heard the words "Odin" and "Earth Spirits". Then he fell silent, stood back and peered into the pot.

'There you are,' he said. 'They've melted and the silver is cleansed. The Rings of Doom are destroyed.'

The flames were dying down. With his bare hands, he lifted the red-hot pot onto a cooling-stone.

'I'll take the remains back to the West Fjords, and bury them there,' he said.

'That won't put *you* in any danger, will it, Chieftain?' said Pa anxiously.

Lygari grunted: 'Most unlikely.' He tipped out the warm lump of silver, went to the porch and slipped it into his saddlebag.

Pa went after him, beaming. He seized the chieftain's hand – not the one with the ugly stump – and shook it very heartily.

'It's funny how things work out, isn't it?' he said. 'I mean, it started off so badly with your horse lost in the floods, and then we misunderstood each other and almost got into a fight. But in the end you've been able to return our good deed to you with an even better one to us. We're really lucky to have you as a friend of the family, Chieftain Lygari – really honoured!'

16

The farmhands came in from the fields, stamping their feet from the cold. The housemaid set up small tables: one by the high-seat, in front of Chieftain Lygari and Pa; two more in front of the family and the farmhands on the opposite side of the fire. Then Ma served up the meal.

There were plenty of stewed blood sausages, hot from the pot, for everyone. There were also big chunks of smoked sheep's head, soured sheep's udders and whole grilled river trout. Sigrid handed round the wooden bowls of food and wooden cups of frothy, sour milk. At last she sat down with her own helping, glancing curiously across at the chieftain.

He had removed his snot-stained face-cloth, laying it in a crumpled heap on the bench beside him; but his face was still hidden by the shadows of his deep hood.

The knife that he unclipped from his belt to cut up the sausages was rusty and heavily stained. He ate fast and greedily.

Ma handed out bowls of yoghurt and sour butter to dip the meat into, and the chieftain rolled up his sleeves to keep them out of the way. Sigrid couldn't help staring at his grotesque finger-stump. Also, his wrists were covered in ugly, bright red burn scars.

Ma nudged her. 'Don't gawp,' she whispered.

Unfortunately, Chieftain Lygari heard. He made a loud *'harrumph'* noise, then held up his hands.

'I'm not a pretty sight, eh?' he said. 'That's because in my youth I was an ignorant fighting man. But I'm wiser now. When idiots bug me these days, I don't bother to beat them up.' His head was turned directly towards Sigrid. 'Instead, I deal with them by playing a clever trick.'

Sigrid peered uselessly into the impenetrable shadows of his hood. 'What...what kind of trick?' she mumbled.

'Oh, it's very simple,' said the chieftain jovially. 'I just lead them into a very lonely part of the desert on a fool's errand – and dump them there. By the time they find their way out, they're in such a state, they never dare to cross me again.' He took a noisy slurp from his mug. 'Remember, girl: that's the way to deal with anyone who gives you trouble.'

Sigrid had a strange sensation, as if his invisible eyes were looking straight into her mind, guessing her most secret and shameful thoughts.

Of course, that's what chieftains do, she reminded herself. *Every year at the Great Thing, they listen to people's excuses when they're accused of crimes, and decide whether or nor they're guilty.*

It was disturbing, sitting in the same room as such a powerful man.

'It's lucky you can't see the scars on my face,' said Lygari. 'They're even worse than my hands.' He gave a spluttering rasp of laughter. 'But don't judge me by my appearance, girl. I am not what I appear to be.'

Sigrid was so embarrassed, she couldn't finish her meal. She sat squirming on the bench, and was relieved when Ma sent her out to the storeroom to help the housemaid wash the dishes.

Magnus helped fold up the tables, then settled down with the men and Ma around the fire.

Chieftain Lygari stretched his arms with a loud sigh and wrapped the cloth back round his face. Bristly strands of greying beard poked out underneath it.

'I could do with a game of King's Table, to help me relax after my long journey,' he said. He turned to Magnus and snapped his fingers. 'Go and fetch my saddlebag from the porch, boy. I've got a fine gaming set in it.'

Magnus jumped up to do the errand like an over-eager slave. Chieftain Lygari drew a soft leather pouch from the bag and tipped its contents onto the bench beside him.

There was a large board, beautifully made from yellowish-white walrus ivory, so highly oiled and polished that it gleamed in the firelight. Its border was carved with entwining stems and galloping horses. In the middle of this were nine-times-nine rows of small holes. Handles protruded from either side, cleverly carved to look exactly like horse heads.

There was also a set of round playing pieces, each with a sharp spike at the bottom, to slot into the holes. Sixteen were made of translucent, orange amber and eight of shiny, black jet. One of the jet pieces was twice the size of the others.

Lygari arranged the playing pieces in their correct places. The black King's Men surrounded the large, black King in the centre. The orange Attackers were grouped around the edge. 'Who's playing against me?' he asked.

The farmhands all grinned sheepishly and shook their heads, reluctant to oppose such an important man.

'Let me play, Pa!' cried Magnus. 'Please, please, please!'

Pa turned to Lygari. 'Would you mind, Chieftain?' he said. 'My son is an excellent player for his age. Not many grown men can beat him.'

Chieftain Lygari beckoned Magnus with a hairy finger. 'Come on then lad, I'll give you a try. Which side will you be: Attackers or King's Men?'

'If I'm really allowed to choose,' said Magnus, 'I'd like to attack.' He sat down on the bench, on the opposite side of the board.

The chieftain grunted and started the game by moving one of the King's Men.

Magnus looked at where he had put it and felt pleased: loads of people made that opening move.

Maybe Chieftain Lygari isn't a particularly good player,

he thought. *Hopefully it'll be easy to impress him.* He took his turn.

The chieftain had another go, just in the way that Magnus guessed he would. And so they played on.

This is as easy as playing against Kari, thought Magnus, with a pang of disappointment. *Ah well, I'll do one of those cunning twisty things anyway, to make sure he sees how clever I am!*

So for his next move, he tried to corner one of the King's Men.

At once the chieftain reacted with a totally unexpected move and swept one of Magnus's Attackers off the board.

Magnus stifled a groan. *Aw,* he thought. *He was just bamboozling me, to catch me unawares!* For the first time, he realised that he might actually lose the game. His heart began to beat very fast.

Magnus didn't make another move for a long time. He huddled over the board, imagining what would happen if he moved in this way...or in that way. How would the chieftain respond? Not as most players would, that was for certain.

The chieftain didn't hurry Magnus. He sat very still, not saying a word. Pa and the farmhands drew closer to watch.

Magnus decided to take a risk. He moved one of his Attackers daringly through four squares, right up to the King itself.

He was really surprised by the chieftain's next few moves. They seemed irrelevant and reckless, losing him two pieces. Then suddenly Lygari placed the King just one square away from one of the corners – one square away from winning!

'AW, DWARF SPIT!' swore Magnus. He saw Ma glaring at him, but he couldn't stop himself. A wave of heat swept through his body and his head throbbed: he could feel one of his rages coming on. 'FARTING, PUKING GIANTESSES!' he yelled. He leaped from his seat and started jumping up and down. 'IT'S NOT FAIR!'

'Be silent!' Chieftain Lygari stood up too, towering over him, waving his finger-stump.

Magnus's eyes glazed over. The colour drained from his face. He slumped back onto the bench.

The chieftain sat down and cleared his throat. Magnus shuddered. Then he turned back to the board and studied it for a long moment. Without a word, he made his next move.

This time it was the chieftain who cursed under his breath.

They had three more goes each – by which time, the tables were turned! Magnus captured another of the chieftain's pieces. Then, with a great flourish, he moved the last Attacker needed to surround the chieftain's King.

'Captured!' Magnus yelled. He leaped from his seat, punching the air and jumping up and down. 'YIPPEE – I've won!'

There was a long silence. Hastily, Magnus slid back onto the bench. He clapped his hand over his mouth and hung his head.

Everyone in the room looked at Chieftain Lygari nervously.

17

But Lygari just roared with laughter and slapped Magnus heartily on the back.

'Well done, boy,' he bellowed in a very friendly way. 'You played brilliantly.'

Magnus felt as if his heart would burst with pride. The only thing that spoiled it was Sigrid standing in the door of the storeroom, scowling at him.

'But don't think you can beat me every time,' the chieftain went on. 'Some day soon we'll play another game, but more seriously – for a prize or a forfeit. Will you accept my challenge?'

'Oh ya, sir, definitely!' said Magnus.

'Excellent.' The chieftain turned to Ma. 'But right now I'd like to go to bed, please, good lady.'

Ma and the housemaid bustled into the storeroom, bringing out great armfuls of bedding: straw mattresses, feather quilts, sheepskins and pillows. Ma made up a comfortable bed on the longest bench for the chieftain. On the opposite bench, Sigrid and Magnus had to squeeze next to Ma and Pa, on one side of the high-seat. The farmhands and the housemaid all huddled together on the other side.

Soon the stuffy room was full of the sound of steady breathing and snoring. The chieftain's snores were loudest of all, rumbling and spluttering like the volcano. Sigrid couldn't stand it. And she was so squashed. And the room was foul and stuffy from the chieftain's revolting, rotten-meat smell. She sat up.

By the red glow of the banked-up fire, she saw Magnus dreaming happily, a smug smile dancing over his lips. She stuck her tongue out at him, glad that Ma couldn't see her.

Then she gazed across the fire-pit to the sleeping chieftain, completely enveloped in his hood and cloak. A queasy feeling wormed its way into her stomach as she recalled his warning about Grim Gruesome.

But there's nothing to worry about, because the chieftain's destroyed the Rings of Doom, she thought. *So Grim Gruesome can't possibly catch us now.*

She lay down again and tried to sleep. Faces came

swimming through her mind: Faithful's – familiar and kindly; Elf's – snow white, eerily beautiful; and then Asny's – spitting and angry, shouting that she didn't want Sigrid as her friend. Tears pricked her eyes.

She blinked them away and forced her thoughts back to Chieftain Lygari. *What was that trick he told me to remember?* The words floated effortlessly back into her head: *Oh, ya: 'When idiots bug me...dump them in the desert...'*

And then she completely stopped worrying about Faithful, Elf and Asny, because she had the most brilliant idea: *I could do that to Magnus!*

She sat there, dead still, gazing into the darkness. *I'd get into terrible trouble,* she thought. *And it's wrong...*

She bit a loose piece of cuticle off her fingernail and spat it onto the floor.

...Or maybe it isn't. If a great chieftain can do it, why shouldn't I? Anyway, I wouldn't be as cruel as Chieftain Lygari. I wouldn't actually leave Magnus out there – I'd just hide from him long enough to give him a big fright, then jump out and bring him safely home.

The night seemed huge with possibilities.

Ma and Pa wouldn't even know. It wouldn't do Magnus any harm... But it might cure him of his nastiness once and for all!

18

Unlike his sister, Magnus didn't have any worries. Instead, he slept soundly through most of the night, and woke up still feeling really pleased with himself.

Fancy me beating a great man like Chieftain Lygari at King's Table! he thought. *Kari and Ref will be so impressed when I tell them.*

He rolled over, sat up and rubbed his eyes. The rest of the family and the servants were all still sound asleep. But the bench on the far side of the fire was empty: Chieftain Lygari had vanished.

He must have made an early start on his long journey back to the West Fjords, thought Magnus.

He threw off his covers and slipped from the bench. He tiptoed round the room to the spot where the chieftain had slept, wrinkling his nose at the lingering rotten-meat smell and grinning to himself.

One day, I'll be a great man like him, he thought. He imagined travelling from farm to farm, being greeted eagerly and fussed over wherever he went. *If I need a bed for the night, people will always give me the comfiest place by the fire, or even a proper bed-cupboard. They'll cook me their finest food, and listen goggle-eyed to my stories; and when I ride away in the morning, all the ladies will weep.*

Then he remembered he had a big problem to overcome before his dream could come true.

If this is really going to happen, I've got to get over my fear of riding. Hmm. He glanced across at Sigrid, who was fidgeting about with her back to him. *She'll help me. Ma will make her, like she always does – because I'm the special one in this family!*

19

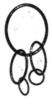

'There's nothing in the least bit special about you, Magnus,' scoffed Sigrid. 'You're a stupid little squirt, and a scaredy-cat. Chieftain Lygari came to reward *me*, not you. He only played King's Table with you because he felt sorry for you.'

They were standing outside, watching a new sprinkling of snow drift down from the grey sky.

'You seem to have forgotten,' said Magnus calmly, 'that *I* organised the rescue of his horse from the river…'

'Liar! You just made a nuisance of yourself. You didn't care about the horse at all. You don't even like horses. Fancy a grown up boy like you being too scared to ride!'

Magnus picked up a handful of snow, shaped it expertly into a ball and chucked it at Sigrid's face, swearing when she ducked just in time.

'Well, it was definitely my idea to bring Chieftain Lygari's horse here,' he said. '*I* was the one who pointed out that we'd get a valuable reward for saving it.'

'Ya, but it was *me* who got the reward,' retorted Sigrid. 'Because *I'm* the one who's so good with horses. Don't you dare make out that Chieftain Lygari's more impressed by you than me!'

'Well, of course he is,' said Magnus. 'Why would a chieftain be interested in a girl? Except, perhaps, to be his slave. Which would be just what you deserve, fish-head!'

Sigrid couldn't contain herself. She slapped Magnus hard.

'*OW!*' he yelled.

Sigrid turned her back on him and raced across the icy ground towards the paddock, where Faithful was standing by the fence, watching her hopefully.

'Sigrid, come here at once!' Ma had suddenly appeared from behind the house. She marched after Sigrid and grabbed her arm. 'You'll get a whipping, my girl, if you don't stop provoking Magnus,' she scolded.

'I only said the truth,' said Sigrid. 'He ought to be ashamed at his age that I have to take him everywhere. And what about *him* provoking *me*, Ma? Last night was the only time in my life that I've been rewarded for doing well – and he has to poke his nose in and steal my glory. It's not fair!'

'You know Magnus is an exceptionally clever boy,' said Ma. 'He's learned over fifty hero-poems off by heart already, he can read runes and he's very knowledgeable about the Great Thing. He did us all proud, beating Chieftain Lygari at King's Table last night. Anyone can see he's going to be successful when he grows up. You won't be complaining when he comes home with a great hoard of treasure, and gives you a share of it, will you?'

20

Spring came. The snow melted and grass grew thickly over the volcanic ash which had polluted Salmon Valley. The air was crisp and clean, and there were masses of white, crimson, blue and yellow wild flowers everywhere. It was as if the eruption had never happened. No wonder everyone at Underhill Farm felt happy!

And who do you think was happiest of all? It was Faithful. For Sigrid had stopped fussing around with Elf and given all her attention back to *him*. Every morning Faithful went racing round the paddock, bucking and squealing loudly to tell the world that life was good again. And then Sigrid would appear with a tasty titbit in her hand, ready to ride him.

True, Sigrid did usually go off with Elf afterwards – but only because she was using the new horse to give

Magnus riding lessons. And, to everyone's surprise, Magnus was riding much better than he'd ever done before. Instead of slithering about in the saddle and wailing with terror, he sat calmly on Elf's back, eyes half closed, nodding as she trotted along to the rhythm of her jangling rattle.

Ma and Pa were both thrilled.

'Elf's a marvellous horse,' said Ma. 'Fancy Magnus being so keen to ride her!'

'Ya,' said Pa. 'And it's good to see Sigrid being so kind to him.'

'So she ought to be!' said Ma. 'I'm sure Magnus is destined for great things.'

'Well, Chieftain Lygari is just the man to show him the way,' said Pa. 'What luck that he's befriended us!'

Of course, like many parents, they didn't have a clue what was really going on.

Although Elf was docile and her rattle had a marvellously soothing effect, Magnus still secretly panicked whenever he rode her.

As for Sigrid… Well, she was helping him for two reasons, but neither had anything to do with kindness.

Firstly, she felt bored and lonely now Asny wasn't her friend any more. And secondly, she needed Magnus to ride so she could carry out her plan – inspired by Chieftain Lygari – and dump him in the wilderness.

We'll ride together to a really lonely spot where he's never been before, she thought. *Then, when he's not looking, I'll gallop away and hide. He'll never dare ride fast enough to catch me up. He's such a baby, he won't dare ride all the way home by himself either! Of course, I won't be as cruel as Chieftain Lygari. I'll only leave Magnus long enough to work himself up into a bad tizzy, and then I'll go back for him.*

She grinned to herself.

But even then, I won't agree to take him home, I'll threaten to leave him there for ever – unless he promises always to be nice to me!

21

Soon it was Sun-Month – high summer. It never gets really hot in Iceland, but the days were long, the sky was blue and the sun was shining.

'Ma,' begged Sigrid, 'please could I have a day off from sewing shoes? I could ride to the Bog Hills and gather some moss there for you.'

"Iceland moss" is a short, pale green plant with soft, curvy fronds like seaweed. Ma often used it to make her cooking extra tasty.

'That would be really helpful,' said Ma, beaming at Sigrid in surprise. 'I've completely run out of it, but I'm so busy with cheese making, I've no time to gather some myself. Can you remember the best place to find it?'

'Of course. You've taken me there loads of times.' Sigrid forced herself to sound cheerful, so Ma wouldn't guess she was up to mischief. 'And I was thinking, Magnus could come too. Then we'd get twice as much moss for you, and it would give him a proper ride on Elf, now he's got his confidence.'

'Oh, you *have* turned into a nice girl, Sigrid!' cried Ma.

Sigrid twiddled her toes inside her shoes guiltily.

'I'm not going with her,' said Magnus.

'Why ever not?' said Ma.

Magnus didn't want to admit that he was still too scared to ride such a long way on Elf. So he cleared his throat and said condescendingly, 'Moss gathering is women's work.'

'No it's not,' said Pa, coming in from the fields to get a drink. 'I often used to do it when I was a boy. Be a good lad, Magnus, and help us out. We don't want Sigrid spending a whole day in the Bog Hills on her own.'

'Listen, Magnus,' said Sigrid, 'On the way to the Bog Hills, we can cross the river at the ford, ride into the desert – and go to see the lava that flowed out when the volcano erupted last year.'

Magnus's eyes lit up. But then it hit him: *That means riding twice as far! I'll never manage it!* His stomach clenched into a tight knot.

'Perhaps you don't want to see the lava after all?' teased Sigrid. 'Or you're too scared to ride such a long way?'

That did it. Magnus swallowed three times, then forced himself to say 'Of course I want to see it! I'll come and help you, Sigrid – if you promise we can see the lava first.'

So far, Sigrid's plan was working perfectly.

Ma and Pa were delighted at how well Sigrid prepared the little expedition.

She persuaded Magnus to take his warmest cloak and a fur hat. She packed a big picnic of wind-dried fish and fatty smoked meat – making sure that Magnus's saddlebag was much fuller than her own – and a big leather flask of water for each of them.

So if my trick keeps us out till late, she thought, *at least I can't be blamed for letting him get cold, hungry or thirsty!*

They set off early the next morning, trotting through the wide valley, past River Bend Farm and several other turf houses, following the River Salmon, with the desert on the far side.

Sigrid led the way on Faithful, Magnus following nervously behind, sweating heavily, clinging to the reins so tightly that his fingernails cut into his palms. *Kringle, kringle!* went the rattle, until the endless jangling began to calm and then mesmerise him. His head nodded. His hands relaxed. His eyelids drooped...

'Oi, wake up!' Sigrid yelled. 'Here's the ford.'

They had reached a fork in the road. The main branch continued straight along the valley. But a smaller track led down to a wide bank of shingle, then right into the river. It was so shallow here that the brown stones at the bottom were clearly visible.

Magnus shook himself awake. He stared across the water, blinking through the wilderness to the distant snow mountains where the volcano stood, sloping down to a wide expanse of hills, streaked with darkness.

'See those black lines?' he said breathlessly. 'They must be the valleys – filled up with lava! I've heard the men say that it pours out the top of the volcano as boiling liquid, then cools down and turns completely solid. We've got to see this before we gather any moss, Sigrid – you promised!'

Sigrid was grinning secretly to herself as she led the way down to the ford. Faithful and Elf stopped there for a long drink, then waded into the cold, grey water. It was fast-rushing, but barely ankle high to a horse, and they soon came up safely on the far side.

Here the track continued into the desert. But they turned off it, for the lava flows lay in a different direction. Magnus was wide awake now and chuckling with excitement as they entered an unmarked landscape of stones and dust.

22

The arid ground was covered in a thick layer of ash and littered with huge lumps of rock. A confusion of low, craggy hills and ridges obscured the view ahead. Smoke swathed the black lava that lay in the valleys. The air was thick with the nauseating stench of bad eggs. There was no sign of life.

The sky clouded over.

The horses picked their way over the uneven ground, lurching and swaying. But for once, Magnus didn't worry at all about falling off, for he was too busy goggling at the scenery.

At last they reached the hills and turned into a narrow valley. They followed a series of bends and forks, passing smaller gulleys on either side, glimpsing banks of lava at the ends.

'We can't take the horses any further,' said Sigrid.

'Well, help me get down then,' said Magnus imperiously.

Sigrid almost yelled at him to do it himself; but she didn't want to waste time arguing. So she let Magnus cling to her like a baby as he slipped awkwardly to the ground.

'I'm a brilliant rider now, aren't I?' said Magnus.

Sigrid bit her tongue. 'Ya, brilliant. Off you go then. Don't be long.'

'Don't rush me! You know how interested I am in volcanoes.'

'Ya, but don't forget we're supposed to be gathering moss for Ma.'

Magnus wasn't listening. He was already running down a gulley towards the lava.

'Don't go too far,' Sigrid called after him, pretending to be concerned.

Magnus quickened his pace, taking nimble leaps and strides over the stony ground, eyes fixed on the smoking landscape. He didn't look round once.

Sigrid stood, hands on hips – just like Ma when she was scolding them – glowering at her brother's back.

You stupid know-all! she thought. *Just you wait till you find I've gone. That'll wipe the smirk off your ugly face!*

107

23

Faithful stood very still, waiting for Sigrid. He didn't like the desert.

He didn't like Elf either. She never ran round the paddock with the other horses. She always just stood silently and submissively, head down, ears low, waiting for one of the humans to make her do things. Faithful swished his tail at her impatiently, then backed away.

Elf turned her head, which set off her irritating rattle again: *Kringle, kringle!*

Faithful rolled his eyes at her and stamped.

Elf ignored him.

Then suddenly Sigrid was jumping onto Faithful's back and pulling urgently at the reins to turn him round. She squeezed him gently with her legs: 'Come on, boy!'

They went back up the valley and emerged into the open desert. There was a hint of rain on the wind. Faithful began to gallop as fast as he could, heading eagerly back to the green farmlands. Once he stopped briefly to turn his head, but there was no sign of Elf and Magnus coming after them.

Faithful was overjoyed to be on his own with Sigrid. And Sigrid was jubilant to be galloping on his back, free of her irritating brother. She laughed out loud as Faithful carried her faster and faster, away from the lowering rain clouds, towards the river and the enticing smell of grass.

24

Magnus was greatly relieved to have his feet on the ground again. Grinning excitedly, he made his way over rocks that were the red-brown colour of vanquished fire. He passed into a haze of smoke, foul with the bad eggs smell, and emerged above a ravine. Here at last he could gaze down directly onto the lava.

It was like a brittle, black, solidified river.

I wonder if it's true, what the old stories say, he thought. *Are there really dwarfs working as blacksmiths inside the mountains? And do volcanoes erupt because they've over-heated their forges?*

He squatted down and reached out gingerly to touch the lava. A glowing warmth seeped into his fingers. Brazenly, he pressed down harder on it…

'OW!'

…And scorched himself. He jumped back.

'Whoo-ee!' he said. 'So this is what it's like!'

He badly wanted to walk across the petrified lava flow, but Ma would be cross if it burned his shoes. So instead, he clambered onto some rocks skirting the edge, and managed to follow it quite a long way up. He kept stopping to marvel at patches that were still glowing red with the heat, or where the smoke rose so thickly that it turned the surroundings invisible.

Suddenly he realised it was drizzling. He looked up and saw a sheet of black cloud blowing towards him.

'Farting giantesses,' he grumbled. 'I'll get soaked unless I fetch my cloak.'

He picked his way back carefully. Elf was still waiting for him in exactly the same spot where he had left her, as if she hadn't even moved an eyelash. There was no sign of Sigrid. But he was too busy wrapping his cloak over his damp tunic and yanking up the hood to worry about her.

The drizzle became a downpour. He spotted a shallow cave, formed by a crack in an overhanging rock, and ran to shelter inside it.

The rainstorm went on and on. Magnus was exhausted from the stress of his long ride and the excitement of the lava-field. He curled up inside the cave and soon dozed off to sleep.

He woke a short time later to find that the wind had blown the storm away. He stepped out gratefully into the watery sunshine and went back to the hollow between the hills where he had started from. Elf was still standing there, motionless – and alone.

'Sigrid!' he yelled crossly. 'Where are you?'

No answer.

She must have gone somewhere else to shelter from the rain, he thought. *Perhaps she fell asleep too.*

He decided to explore some more. He retraced his steps and spent ages squatting over the lava and examining it in detail, pondering on dwarfs and fires. Then he climbed up some rocks to gaze at the distant mountains, trying to work out which one was the volcano. But whichever it was, it looked exactly the same as all the other mountains now. It was hard to believe that only last year it had been spewing out smoke and flames.

At last he felt satisfied. He made his way back, expecting Sigrid to greet him in a fury for keeping her waiting.

But she still wasn't there.

'Sigrid,' he yelled crossly. 'Stop playing pathetic games and come here!'

No answer. No sign of her.

I know, he thought. *Her stupid old horse always comes when she calls him, so maybe he'll come for me too.*

He cupped his hands and shouted: 'Faithful, come here, boy! FAITHFUL!'

Silence.

He began to get worried.

'Sigrid, come here, you stupid, pig-faced piece of poo! If you don't come, I'll...I'll go home without you!'

But he couldn't help thinking: *I dare not ride home by myself! Who will help me if I fall off?* A lump of fear rose in his throat. He gulped it back. *Anyway, I'm not sure if I know the way. We kept turning round rocks and ridges...but I felt so drowsy – I'll never remember where they were – especially going in the opposite direction. Flaming sheep poo!*

'Sigrid!' he yelled. 'Just you wait till I tell Ma and Pa that you've been hiding from me. They'll give you such a whipping, you won't be able to sit down for months!'

Still, nothing.

She's gone, he thought. *Abandoned me.*

He spun round, expecting her to leap out from somewhere shouting 'Here I am, fish-head!' But it didn't happen.

There was a rocky ledge just behind Elf, rather like a bench. He sat down on it and made himself think.

The first thing he worked out was that he was hungry. So he went to see what was in his saddlebag – and was more than pleased to find all the food Sigrid had packed for him.

Of course she hasn't abandoned me, he thought, chewing gratefully on a big dried fish. *She always looks after me, just like Ma tells her to. The idiot's probably got lost herself.*

He climbed onto the rocks and shouted for her again, hoping that the wind would carry his voice further from up there.

But there was still no answer.

He fetched another dried fish from Elf's saddlebag and sat down again.

I'm on my own, he thought. He took a deep breath.

'But I'm not going to panic,' he said out loud. 'A chieftain would never panic, no matter what. I just need to devise a sensible plan. Then everything will work out fine.'

25

Leaving the rain clouds behind, Faithful carried Sigrid back to the river at a gallop and splashed through the ford. As soon as he reached the other side, he gave a happy whinny and started tearing up mouthfuls of grass.

'We won't hurry back, boy,' said Sigrid, patting his neck. 'I need to give Magnus plenty of time to work himself up into a proper panic. Anyway, the Bog Hills are just close by – we might as well go there now, and get the moss collected.'

Soon Faithful was grazing contentedly as Sigrid wandered through the damp grass and flowers, tearing up clumps of moss and stuffing it into her sack.

When she was done, she fixed the full sack onto Faithful's saddle. Then she re-crossed the ford and rode back into the volcanic wastelands.

She gazed at the vast plain, the distant uplands and valleys, all formed of bare sand, rock, stone and ash. It was completely barren and colourless, forbidding and utterly bleak.

She had intended to make a mental note of exactly where she had left Magnus. But in the exhilaration of her gallop, these good intentions had flown straight out of her mind. Now she saw that there were loads and loads of lava flows, jutting out wherever there was a gap between the hills. There were no obvious differences between them.

Which one did I take Magnus to? she wondered. *Hmm. It must have been the nearest one.*

But several of the lava flows looked equally near.

Wasn't it somewhere in the middle? I reckon...Ya, it was over there.

She set off for a deep gulley with a large fuzz of smoke hanging over it.

However, she didn't really recognise any of the boulders and rock formations that she passed on the way. And when she finally reached it, there was no sign of Magnus or Elf.

She didn't want to shout for Magnus, because the whole point of her trick was that *he* should be anxiously looking for *her.* So she and Faithful slipped behind an outcrop of rock to hide until he turned up.

But he didn't.

Sigrid waited and waited. She grew crosser and crosser.

This is so typical of him! she thought. *Just when I work out a brilliant plan to deal with him once and for all — the little brat has to spoil it!*

She sat there fuming, planning how to keep the upper hand when Magnus finally turned up. And then she noticed something.

That's strange, she thought. *There was definitely a rocky ledge above the lava flow before, wide enough to walk on. I saw Magnus climb onto it. So where is it?*

Her anger began to drain away. She felt a chill of fear.

Anyway, where's Elf? Magnus wouldn't dare ride her without me to help him. And she never wanders off…

Her heart was beating very fast.

Freyja's tears! I don't think this is the right place!

She retraced her steps to the desert plain, then rode as fast as she could to a different lava-filled gulley.

But Magnus wasn't there either.

Sigrid bit her lip so hard it began to bleed. She

117

galloped almost back to the river. There she made herself carefully inspect the whole landscape, from one end of the uplands to the other. The air was so clear, she could see for miles.

It was totally confusing. The countless petrified flows of lava all looked identical.

'How am I supposed to remember which is the right one?' she wailed. 'I'll never find him! Oh, oh, why ever didn't I watch where I was going?'

She burst into tears.

Then a new thought hit her. *Supposing something dreadful happens to Magnus?* She imagined him lost and forlorn in the middle of nowhere, whimpering like a toddler, waiting in vain for her to come back.

The wilderness was overwhelming. The pit of her stomach began to ache and flutter. *I'll have to go home without him! I can't bear it! And what am I going to tell Ma?*

Tears streamed down her face.

Eventually she started wretchedly for home. However, she didn't get very far before her heart sank even more. For three very odd-looking figures were coming along the road towards her, waddling like over-fed geese.

Oh no! thought Sigrid. *It's those weird old witch women who called at the farm last year.*

It was impossible to avoid them: the women had already spotted her. They quickened their pace, waving madly.

Supposing they guess what I've done? thought Sigrid. *Supposing they tell Ma and Pa?*

'What good luck, sisters – it's really her!' cried scraggy Helga as they drew level. 'Sigrid, my dear! We're so glad to find you. We called at your house, but no one was home.' Her toothless, sunken mouth was twisted into a delighted grin.

Tall, stooped Vigdis sniffed and wiped her warty nose on the edge of her cloak. 'We came to say thank you for the shoes.'

Sigrid managed to find her voice. 'Oh. Um, are they all right?'

'Ya, surprisingly enough, they're very well made,' said fat Groa grudgingly.

'We've been wearing them ever since you gave them to us,' said Helga, 'but they've hardly worn out at all. And they're ever so comfy.'

Groa nodded. 'We misjudged you, girl. You're kinder than we thought.'

A picture of Magnus, abandoned and terrified in the desert, flashed into Sigrid's mind. 'Oh no,' she blurted. 'I...I'm not kind at all!'

'Nonsense, dear, of course you are,' Helga insisted. 'Not many folk are willing to help three grumpy old battle-axes like us! We'd like to give you something in return.'

'As you know, we haven't got anything valuable' said Groa, wobbling her double chins. 'But we found this lying in the road the other day and we thought it might be useful to you.' She shoved Vigdis with her elbow. 'Give it to her, sister,' she hissed.

Vigdis stooped even lower than usual. She fumbled awkwardly under her cloak and pulled out a metal object as long as her hand, attached to a short chain. It was thin and flat, with a rough edge. She dropped it into Sigrid's palm, closing her fingers around it.

'Er...what is it?' said Sigrid.

'Hook the chain onto your brooch straightaway, girl, so you don't lose it,' said Groa sternly. 'It's a file, of course.'

It looked more like a man's tool of some kind, much too big and heavy to file her nails. But to avoid trouble, Sigrid thanked the women politely and did as she was told.

She was about to say goodbye and ride on, when Helga said, 'Wait, dear. We've got some important news. Remember what we told you last time, about those evil Rings of Doom?'

To tell the truth, Sigrid had almost forgotten about them. 'Oh, those,' she said impatiently. 'A chieftain told us what they are – but that was ages ago. He said they're connected with that villain – you know, Grim Gruesome – the child killer.' She was gabbling, anxious to get away from the women. 'And someone gave me a set of really lovely silver rings – but the chieftain said they were very suspicious – that *they* might be the Rings of Doom. Anyway, it all turned out fine, because he destroyed them for us.'

Vigdis bristled her eyebrows. 'That chieftain didn't know what he was talking about!' she snorted. 'He was right about Grim Gruesome, of course. But your gift couldn't possibly be the Rings of Doom.' She stepped closer, stooping right over Sigrid and Faithful, and lowered her voice. 'We stayed recently at a farm where the old grandfather was very clever at interpreting dreams. He revealed the truth about our nightmares. He told us what the Rings of Doom really are.'

'They're not jewellery, Sigrid,' said Helga loudly. 'They're *horse*-rings.'

Sigrid felt as if someone had punched her in the stomach. 'What...what are horse-rings?' she whispered. But she had already guessed the answer.

'You know,' said Groa disapprovingly. 'Those noisy rattles that show-offs hang from their horses' bridles to make sure everyone knows they're coming.'

'So mind you keep away from any horses wearing rattles, Sigrid dear,' said Helga. 'Then that horrible Grim Gruesome will never get hold of *you*!'

'Come on now, sisters,' said Groa. 'We must be on our way.'

'Bye-bye, Sigrid!' Helga blew her a kiss as the three women waddled off. 'And thank you again for the shoes!'

26

Sigrid imagined the evil Grim Gruesome battering Magnus with Elf's rattle, mocking him for not realising that *they* were the Rings of Doom. She longed for a reason not to believe what Groa, Helga and Vigdis had told her. And as she rode on, she found one:

Lygari said ALL chieftains' horses wear rattles, she thought. *So how can they possibly be the Rings of Doom? Those old hags don't know what they're saying! I'm not going to worry about it any more. I need to concentrate on what to tell Ma and Pa when they ask where Magnus is.*

She agonised over this for the rest of the way home, her stomach mangled into a sickly knot of misery. At last she came up with a convincing excuse.

'Magnus stopped off at River Bend Farm on the way back,' she told Ma. 'He's promised to teach Kari how to read and write runes. He said he'll probably stay over there tonight. And maybe tomorrow night too...'

Ma was so busy with her cheese making that she just nodded vaguely. She was really pleased with Sigrid's big sackful of moss.

All evening, all night, Sigrid was on tenterhooks, wriggling about as if she had fleas. *Please, mighty Thor,* she prayed silently. *Please help Magnus to find his way home safely!*

She hardly ate. She couldn't sleep.

The next morning, Pa started grumbling because Magnus wasn't there to help on the farm. But Ma retorted that he should be proud of their son's ability to teach his friend something so clever. Neither of them was concerned by his absence.

'It's lovely and peaceful without you two constantly arguing,' Ma said cheerfully. 'Perhaps Magnus should stay with Kari more often. I tell you what, Sigrid, you've been such a good and helpful girl recently...'

If only she knew the truth! thought Sigrid wretchedly.

'...So leave your sewing for a few days,' said Ma. 'Go out in the fresh air and enjoy yourself.'

Sigrid longed to ride over to River Bend Farm to

share her problems with Asny. But ever since their big argument, both girls had refused to speak to each other. So she saddled Faithful forlornly and set off for a lonely ride by herself.

She trotted down Salmon Valley, past the hot pool and several other farms, trying not to imagine Magnus lost in the desert. But it was impossible. *Supposing he's slipped on the rocks, or got burned on the lava!* she thought. *There's hardly any water in the desert – he might die of thirst!*

Ahead, the road bent sharply round a high outcrop of rock. A familiar noise suddenly came drifting round it:

Kringle, kringle!

Faithful raised his head, flicked his ears and stopped.

It's Elf! thought Sigrid. *She must have crossed back over the river somewhere downstream.* She felt faint with relief – tinged with apprehension.

Magnus will be in a terrible rage with me – he'll tell Ma and Pa what I did to him... And they'll be horrified. Oh well, I don't care how hard they whip me, so long as he's safe!

Then she had another horrible thought. *Supposing*

she's come back without Magnus? She bit her lip, bracing herself for disappointment.

The next moment, the other horse came into view. It wasn't Elf, after all; it was the great black stallion Haski. And riding him was Chieftain Lygari.

'Sigrid!' he exclaimed. 'Excellent! The very girl I was looking for.'

'Oh, good day to you, sir!' Sigrid flustered about awkwardly, trying to smooth her tangled hair and hide her grubby apron. She felt herself going bright red. Her heart thumped uncontrollably.

Faithful stepped backwards. The chieftain leaned forward, snatched the reins from Sigrid's hands and pulled them towards him. Faithful whinnied indignantly.

The chieftain dismounted and ordered Sigrid to do likewise. They stood so close that his pungent, rotten-meat smell almost overwhelmed her. Haski towered over them, nosing Faithful away, closing in on Sigrid's other side.

The chieftain wasn't wearing a face-cloth now. In the shadows of his deep hood, she caught a glimpse of a grey-flecked, bristly beard. There was also something grotesque – Ugh! It looked like a loose eyeball –

dangling down his cheek on a thread. He said, 'I want a little talk with you, Sigrid.'

'What... What about?' she whispered. Her knees were wobbling so badly, she could scarcely stand. *He must have found out what I've done*, she thought. *He's come to punish me!*

But the chieftain didn't sound angry. He said, 'Remember when I stayed at your house last winter, my dear, and I made you a promise? As well as my gift to you of a horse, I promised you a wonderful surprise.'

Sigrid twisted her fingers and nodded nervously.

'Well now, I've come to tell you the surprise,' Chieftain Lygari continued jovially. 'I am going to make your special wish come true, Sigrid. You know what I mean: your wish about Magnus.'

'Oh, sir!' she cried. 'You know what's happened then? How did you find out?' She was in such a state, she couldn't help dribbling as the words came spilling out. 'Please don't tell me off – I never meant to lose him like that! You must know how much I wish that he could come home safely. Please, please let the surprise be that you've found him, sir!

'I don't think you quite understand me,' said the

chieftain. Suddenly he didn't sound so friendly: his voice had turned rather rough, and icy cold. 'I am referring to a different wish – to the one you have made over and over again.' He paused. 'I mean, your wish to get rid of Magnus.'

Sigrid's mouth dropped open. 'Oh! No, sir, I've never *really* wished that. I only say horrid things about Magnus sometimes as a joke. I mean, he's my *brother*. I love him. I'd never do anything evil…'

'Wouldn't you?' growled Chieftain Lygari.

Sigrid froze. Her throat went so dry, she could scarcely swallow. 'I don't understand,' she croaked. 'You don't mean that… *You're* not going to get rid of him, are you, sir? Oh, sorry, excuse me, I shouldn't have said that, of course you wouldn't. You're a chieftain…'

'Wouldn't I?' he said. ' Am I? What is my name, Sigrid?'

'L…Lygari, sir,' she whispered.

'And what other word means exactly the same as "lygari"?'

It came to her at once. But she thought, *That's impossible!* She shook her head.

'Come now,' he said. 'Let us get this over with. Tell me!'

'"Lygari", she whispered. 'That means…"liar".'

'Well done. So now you know. I am, indeed, a liar, Sigrid. Everything you thought you knew about me is untrue.'

He pulled off his gloves. His bare hands were huge and hairy, with blue, knotted veins standing out under the skin, and ugly burn scars on the wrists. His scab-covered finger-stump was oozing a yellow bubble of pus.

'You and your family are idiots, Sigrid,' he rasped. 'I gave you so many clues. I kept my face hidden. I told you a false name – a ridiculous name – which you should all have seen through at once. Yet your mother and father welcomed me into your house and let me befriend you and Magnus. They feasted me and honoured me.'

He began to wave his finger-stump about: to and fro, to and fro, like a slimy, writhing slug.

'Surely you realise by now who I really am,' he hissed. 'Go on, you pathetic girl: what is my true name?'

Sigrid felt light-headed. She couldn't take her eyes off the stump. Everything was spinning.

'Are you…?' She swayed, reaching out desperately,

clinging to Faithful's mane. 'Surely you're not... You can't be...*Grim Gruesome*?'

She never heard his answer. For the next moment, her head exploded with the sound of thunder, the distant mountains came crowding in on her and the ground fell upwards. Then everything went black.

27

At around the time that Sigrid was gathering moss, Magnus was inspecting his wilderness surroundings and thinking hard. Fortunately, he wasn't the sort of boy to feel sorry for himself, and he soon blanked Sigrid right out of his mind. *I have much more important things to deal with,* he told himself.

The hollow where he stood was a confusing muddle of similar-looking rocks and openings. However, Magnus prided himself on his good memory. After gazing around for a few moments, he felt sure of his bearings and set off down a gulley, chattering cheerfully to himself:

'Here's the way back to the main valley. Once I reach that, I'll soon be out of the hills, and then the river's just across the desert plain.'

He trudged along determinedly, Elf's rattle jingling

as she plodded behind him. He chose confidently between alternative routes when necessary and stayed calm when a dead end forced him to retrace his steps. He balanced much better on solid ground than on horseback, scrambling nimbly over the loose stones.

However, after a while, he began to feel a little worried. *I should be back in the main valley by now,* he thought. Instead, he seemed to have gone deeper than ever into the hills.

He stopped for a rest, sipping stingily from his leather flask and nibbling just a tiny morsel of food from his saddlebag. *Mustn't use up my supplies,* he thought. *Who knows how long they'll have to last?* In some ways he found his situation quite exciting – like a travellers' tale he'd once heard, of men exploring unknown lands far across the sea.

He resumed his trek, this time in a new direction, Elf still following him tirelessly. They continued like this for some time: walk then rest, walk then rest, on and on and on... But they still didn't reach the desert plain.

Twilight fell, heralding the brief summer's night. The wind whistled through the emptiness and shadows flitted spookily across the rock crevasses.

By now Magnus's exhausted legs could scarcely carry him and he couldn't keep his eyes open. Without even thinking about it, he sank down on the spot and dozed off.

He jolted awake as dawn broke.

His first thought was: *I'm lost!*

He staggered up. Despair pricked his heart...then quickly turned to rage.

'FARTING, FLABBY-BOTTOMED GIANTESSES!' he screamed. 'IT'S NOT FAIR! FLAMING, STINKY SHEEP POO! IT'S ALL SIGRID'S FAULT! I HATE HER!'

The tantrum cleared his head, and once he had calmed down, he found himself thinking much more clearly. He pulled himself together and set off, full of confidence once more.

After he had covered quite a distance, he spotted another cave. It looked like a good place to shelter from the wind for a while. He crawled into it, curled up inside his cloak and managed to fall into a deep slumber.

It was well into the afternoon when he finally woke up – disturbed by clattering hooves and a jangling rattle.

He peered blearily out of the cave, wondering what Elf was up to. But she was just standing motionless, as usual.

Then it must be another horse, thought Magnus. *I bet Ma's sent Sigrid to find me – and she's so annoyed, that she's tied together a string of nails or something to try and confuse me. How pathetic!*

Out loud, he shouted: 'Come on then, poo-face, show yourself!'

The horse rounded the rocks and picked its way over the stones towards him...

...And Magnus almost died of embarrassment. For it wasn't Sigrid after all. It was Chieftain Lygari.

28

Magnus crawled out of the cave, heart pounding, blinking at the sunlight. *Everyone makes mistakes,* he thought nervously. *Apologise straightaway, and hopefully he'll let you off.*

He smoothed his crumpled tunic, stood up straight and marched boldly across to meet the chieftain.

'Good day, sir,' He forced himself to speak in a loud, clear voice. 'I'm sorry if I sounded rude just now. Obviously, I wasn't expecting to meet you here. When I heard a horse, I thought it was my sister. She's caused me a lot of trouble. That's why, I'm afraid, I lost my temper.'

The sun was suddenly blotted out by a thick bank of cloud. The chieftain dismounted. Magnus peered up at his towering figure, trying unsuccessfully to make out his face under the shadows of his hood. Lygari said nothing.

He must be waiting for me to explain what I'm doing here, thought Magnus. *Well, best say as little as possible. I'm certainly not admitting that I'm lost, and too scared to ride Elf by myself!* He took a deep breath. *I need to be cunning – get him to show me the way home, without looking pathetic.*

He said carefully, 'Would you care to ride back to Underhill Farm with me, sir? My mother and father would be very pleased to see you again.'

'Don't be ridiculous!' snapped Chieftain Lygari. 'I'm a very busy man, Magnus. I'm on my way to carry out some urgent business.'

'Ya, of course,' said Magnus quickly. 'Um, which way are you going, sir? If you're crossing the ford over the River Salmon, may I ride there with you? I really enjoyed talking to you that night you stayed at our house, and there are lots more things I'd like to discuss.'

'I am not leaving the wilderness, but going much deeper into it,' said Lygari. 'I am on my way to the Racing Sands, as a raven flies, directly over the Water Glacier.'

'Farting…excuse me sir!… I mean, er…thunderbolts! That sounds like a fantastic adventure! I wish I could come with you.'

'Fool!' said Chieftain Lygari. 'Such a journey is much too perilous for a young boy like you.'

'I'm actually older than I look,' said Magnus. 'Pa says he was small at my age too, and I'll probably shoot up any time now, like he did. Please let me come with you, sir! I'd love to see that glacier… Isn't it the biggest one in Iceland? How will you cross it? Could I manage it without skis or snowshoes? I'm very steady on my feet, I never slip over in the snow or anything…'

'Stop this pathetic, girlish chitter-chatter,' said Chieftain Lygari. 'If you realised what terrible things lie ahead, you would not wish to come anywhere with me. Go home, Magnus.'

Terrible things? thought Magnus. *Ya, it will be terrible for me, having to ride all that way.* His stomach churned violently at the thought of it. *But I've GOT to manage it – I can't miss such a fantastic chance!*

Out loud he said, 'Will you be passing any boiling mud-pools, sir?'

The chieftain rubbed his great hands together. 'Ya,' he said softly. 'There are many scalding hot mud-pools on the way to the Water Glacier. No doubt, you will now claim that you've always longed to see such things, and nag me even more to take you.'

Magnus blushed and nodded.

'Your parents will worry if you don't return home,' said Chieftain Lygari.

'I don't care,' said Magnus. 'I'll blame my sister.'

'You do not realise the risk you would be taking,' said Chieftain Lygari. 'How can I persuade you to change your mind?'

'You can't,' said Magnus. 'I hope to be a chieftain too, some day, sir. I realise I need lots of experience of the world first, and this seems an ideal opportunity to get started. Please, please let me come.'

'Very well,' said Chieftain Lygari. 'You may. But you have only yourself to blame, Magnus, if you don't emerge from this adventure alive.'

29

Magnus was determined to get over his fear of riding once and for all. He made himself clamber onto Elf's saddle quickly and without any fuss. When Chieftain Lygari set off, Magnus immediately followed close behind. He kept up with the chieftain's brisk pace, all through the maze of slopes, lava flows and gulleys. And he forced himself to stay calm, muttering: 'I am NOT going to fall off!' until he really believed it.

Eventually they emerged on the far side of the hills, in an area of flat, open desert. Haski broke into a gallop – and at once, Elf began to gallop too. Magnus had never ridden even half as fast before! He opened his mouth to scream…but managed not to.

They sped through a dreary expanse of colourless pebbles and dust, mountains and hills looming on either side through the mist. Magnus clung on fiercely, concentrating with all his might on the mesmerising jingle of the two horses' rattles – *Kringle, kringle! Kringle, kringle!* He began to feel drowsy – almost dropped the reins – jerked awake just before he slipped out of the saddle – then drifted again into a mindless trance. On and on they raced, Magnus dozing and waking fitfully, on and on...

The wind whistled across the desert. It began to grow dark.

They halted at last by a small stream gushing through some rocks, and took a long drink of icy water. Some cow hides and curved wooden poles were roped to Haski's saddle. The chieftain unlashed these and set them up to form a tent. Then he pulled a large joint of meat and bone from his voluminous saddlebag and began chomping on it ravenously.

Ugh! thought Magnus. *That looks raw... And creeping with maggots!* He had to sidle right away before he could bear to eat a morsel of dried fish from his own rations. He was too exhausted to talk.

The horses wandered off to graze on a narrow strip of grass and flowers between the desert and the stream. The chieftain finished his meal and belched loudly. Then he unpacked his shiny King's Table board.

He sat down on a boulder, balanced the board on his enormous knees, and beckoned Magnus to help him set out the orange and black playing pieces. As Magnus rammed the spikes into the holes, he noticed with a shiver how sharp they were.

'Why do you think I agreed to let you travel with me, Magnus?' the chieftain said.

'To show me things, sir?' said Magnus eagerly. 'To teach me things?'

'No, you swollen-headed piece of scum,' the chieftain growled. 'It is so I can play another game with you – and beat you as soundly as you deserve.'

Magnus perched on the boulder – not too close to the chieftain – fidgeting and giggling nervously as he clutched one handle of the board. *He's only teasing, because he was so impressed at me winning last time,* Magnus thought. *Hmm. Perhaps I can persuade him to give me a piece of silver if I win again...*

'Shall we play for a prize this time, sir?' he suggested.

'What prize can you offer me?' the chieftain mocked him.

'Nothing valuable,' admitted Magnus. 'But my sister packed me lots of delicious fatty smoked meat that I've hardly touched. You could have it all, sir… *If you win of course, ha, ha!'*

'Why would I want a simpering girl's snippet of tasteless food?' snapped the chieftain. 'No we will not play for a prize. Instead, whichever of us loses most out of three games must pay a forfeit.'

'That sounds fun,' said Magnus. 'I often gamble on forfeits with my friends.'

'You will find my forfeit more challenging than those you are used to,' said the chieftain drily. 'Now then, let us begin. I shall play Attackers this time. So you must play King's Men – and make the first move.'

The day had almost completely faded to a thin, blue dreg of light. The wind sharpened. They both bent over the gaming board.

Magnus won the first game.

The chieftain made no comment. He set up the playing pieces again.

The chieftain won the second game.

Magnus wasn't in the least bit worried. In fact, he deliberately hadn't played well that time, thinking that the chieftain might be annoyed if he didn't win any games at all.

I'll definitely win the last one, Magnus thought. He

grinned smugly. *So I'd better come up with a really clever forfeit… Nothing that might offend him... Something funny, perhaps…?*

He was so distracted by this, that he didn't pay proper attention to the third game.

Oh no! he realised suddenly. *He's got all my pieces under siege! I'll have to do one of those twiddly moves to escape…*

In moments he had worked out a brilliant strategy for his next two turns. But it was too late.

'Cornered!' Lygari shouted. 'I have won again!'

Magnus was devastated. However, he knew it was important to take defeat with good grace.

'Oh, well done, sir!' he said. He stood up to shake the chieftain's hand, like Pa did with his friends after games of King's Table. But the chieftain just slapped his hand away.

'Now you must pay a forfeit, Magnus,' he said softly. 'I hope you are very afraid.'

'Oh, I'm not, sir,' said Magnus brazenly.

'Then you are even more of a fool than I thought,' said Lygari. 'For tomorrow I shall order you to do something so gross, you will wish with all your heart that you had never set eyes on me, let alone dared play me at this game!'

30

Sigrid opened her eyes. Faithful was standing over her, nostrils quivering, making soft, worried nickering noises. Her head was full of stabbing pains and she felt weak and achy, as if she were going down with a bad cold.

Grim Gruesome had vanished.

She staggered to her feet. Faithful pricked his ears forward and nuzzled her. She sobbed into his mane, then climbed shakily onto his back and rode home.

There was no one around when she arrived. Pa and the farmhands had gone to the sheep hills, and Ma was shut away in a shed with the housemaid, making butter.

'I'm not going to disturb her,' she told Faithful. 'She'll never believe that Chieftain Lygari is really...' she shuddered. '...really Grim Gruesome.'

Faithful snorted sympathetically.

Sigrid couldn't stop crying. 'Oh, oh, how ever can I save poor Magnus? Who can I ask to help me – without getting into even worse trouble?'

She crept into the deserted house and fetched a drink from the barrel of sour milk. After a few sips, she found herself thinking a little more clearly:

Asny would believe me. That night we argued, she said then there was something weird about Chieftain Lygari. Why ever didn't I listen to her?

She blew her nose on a corner of her apron and gulped down the rest of her drink.

And Asny always knows what to do – like when we pulled the horse out of the river. If only she would talk to me!

Suddenly a thought struck her.

Even though Asny hates my guts, she'll want to save Magnus. So will Ref. And Kari is Magnus's best friend. So maybe…?

She had vowed never to grovel to Asny, never to apologise to her. *But who else can I turn to?*

Her mind was made up. She rode at a gallop to River Bend Farm.

The door to the farmhouse was wide open to let in the fresh summer air. Sigrid could see Asny inside, working at the weaving loom. Faithful whinnied, bringing two of the farm dogs bounding out to lick Sigrid's hands. But Asny didn't get up. Instead, her mother came to the door.

'Asny doesn't want to see you,' she said.

Sigrid bit her lip, patted the dogs sadly and sloped off.

Perhaps I can catch Asny when she pops outside to use the bog-hole, she thought. This was in a separate turf-walled shed next to the farmhouse. She set Faithful to graze and sat down on the damp grass, choking back her tears.

As she huddled there, Ref and Kari came up from the river, carrying some fish they had just caught. Kari spat when he saw her, and darted away. But the older boy stopped.

'Ref!' she called. 'Something terrible's happened!'

He hesitated, then reluctantly came and squatted beside her. 'What's up?'

Sigrid told him everything. When she described abandoning Magnus in the desert, Ref swore and slapped her face. But when she described Chieftain Lygari's revelation that he was really the evil Grim Gruesome, his mouth dropped open in astonishment.

'Grim Gruesome?' he cried. 'Here, in Iceland? Surely not!'

'It's true,' sobbed Sigrid. 'And you know those three weird women that Magnus and I met last year? I bumped into them on the way home yesterday. They said they've found out what the Rings of Doom are. Not the top of a volcano, or that jewellery that a stranger gave me, like Magnus thought. They're horse rattles.'

'Odin's eye socket!' swore Ref. 'The chieftain's horse – Grim Gruesome's horse! – wears a rattle on its bridle. And so does the horse he gave you – the one that's with Magnus in the desert.'

'Exactly,' wept Sigrid. 'It must be a trap. Grim Gruesome's probably used it to catch Magnus!'

Ref stood up. 'We need to act quickly.'

'Don't tell your parents,' begged Sigrid. 'They'd tell mine what I did, and Ma would whip me black and blue – kick me out – sell me as a slave! Please don't involve any adults.'

Ref looked doubtful.

'You're nearly a man, Ref,' said Sigrid. 'You're strong enough to fight Grim Gruesome. I could sneak out my pa's sword for you.'

'You must be joking,' said Ref quickly. 'They say that even the fiercest warriors can't beat Grim Gruesome.'

'Then...get Asny to help,' begged Sigrid. 'She won't speak to me... But she always has the best ideas. Please, Ref.'

Ref scratched his head. 'She's still furious with you,' he said. 'But once our ma's out of the way, I'll try to persuade her.'

Sigrid waited and waited. She bit her nails right down to the skin. She crouched underneath Faithful to shelter from a shower of rain. She watched a flock of honking geese fly towards the distant mountains. At last Ref came back, with his sister trailing behind.

'Asny,' said Sigrid in a very small voice. 'I'm sorry...sorry...sorry!'

Asny glowered at her. 'Sshh,' she said coldly. 'I'm thinking.' She turned her back, twisting a strand of hair round her fingers, frowning with concentration.

'Should we go back to where Sigrid fainted this morning and follow Grim Gruesome's tracks from there?' suggested Ref.

'That would waste valuable time,' said Asny. 'We need to assume he's captured Magnus already, and work out his *next* move. What do we know about Grim Gruesome?'

'They say he doesn't kill his victims straightaway,' said Ref bleakly. 'Apparently he always spins things out, torturing them first.'

Sigrid choked back a loud sob.

'Then there's a chance of reaching Magnus while he's still alive,' said Asny. 'Right. So *how* might Grim Gruesome torture him? And where is he most likely to do it?'

'I KNOW!'

They all spun round as Kari suddenly sprang out from behind a rock. 'Why didn't you ask me, Ref?'

'This is really dangerous,' said Ref. 'You're too young to be involved.'

'But Magnus is *my* friend,' said Kari. He spat at Sigrid again, and pulled a face at her. 'I heard everything. I know what you did. I hope your ma *does* whip you – until you're all covered in blood. And then I hope Grim Gruesome gobbles *you* up instead of Magnus!'

'Leave off her,' said Asny half-heartedly.

'I can guess exactly where Grim Gruesome would take Magnus,' crowed Kari. 'They say that he likes to *eat* children, don't they? And that he likes to cook them first.'

'No!' shrieked Sigrid.

'It's no good being squeamish,' Kari sneered. 'If he's planning to cook someone round here, it's obvious where he'll do it.'

The others looked at him blankly.

'The Fiery Holes,' he said.

31

The other children would have been horrified if they had known what Magnus was up to. For not only had he volunteered – no, *begged* – to go off with Grim Gruesome (not realising who he really was, of course), but he was also having the time of his life!

He was thrilled when Chieftain Lygari let him sleep in a corner of his tent. Magnus had often camped before, helping Ma, Pa and the farmhands round up the sheep from the hills at the end of the summer; but that was for namby-pambies, with a layer of heather to soften the tent floor, and thick sheepskin sleeping-sacks. Chieftain Lygari didn't bother with such comforts, but slept directly on the stones and jagged rocks; and for warmth, he simply wrapped his cloak around him. Magnus copied him eagerly.

This is a proper man's life! he thought. He felt really

good, really proud of himself. *I bet Kari and Ref couldn't survive so well in the wilderness. What a shame they can't see me now – they'd be so impressed!*

He rolled over onto his side, listening to the whistling wind and the chieftain's thunderous grunts and snores. *I wonder if he'll let me do the whole journey...and then travel back to the West Fjords with him afterwards, and stay in his house?*

He chuckled excitedly. *Then next year, perhaps he'll take me to the Great Thing. What fantastic training it'll be for becoming a chieftain myself!*

He wasn't at all worried about the forfeit he had to pay. *It's only a game,* he thought, *and Lygari knows I haven't got anything valuable to give him. I'm sure the forfeit will just be a bit of fun.*

With that, Magnus fell asleep and, despite the hard ground and the cold, he didn't wake until the morning. He peered outside at the colourless landscape. The chieftain was already up, prowling around outside, his huge cloak billowing in the wind.

Magnus used a hollow behind a rock as a bog-hole, then went down to splash his hands and face in the icy stream. He was just nibbling a bit of smoked meat from his saddlebag, when the sun came out from behind the clouds – and Lygari's shadow fell over him.

'I've decided your forfeit, boy,' he said.

'Oh good, sir,' said Magnus brightly. 'What is it?

'Yesterday we talked about boiling mud-pools,' said Lygari. 'As you may know, they are intensely hot, and constantly bursting and spattering up... Like this.'

He held up his left hand. Slowly he squeezed the festering stump where his little finger was missing. A bubble of thick, yellow, rancid smelling pus popped out of it, then dribbled across his skin.

Magnus stopped himself from giggling just in time.

'You will soon experience their power for yourself,' the chieftain went on. 'Because your forfeit for losing the games against me, Magnus, is to plunge into a mud-pool, and stay submerged in it until you are thoroughly cooked.'

Magnus stared up into the dark shadows of Lygari's hood for a long moment. He wasn't sure how he should react. *He's testing my courage*, he thought. *I mustn't be unnerved by it.*

In the end he decided that the safest thing was to take this horrific threat in the way it was surely intended.

So he burst out laughing.

Magnus was determined to do everything he could to gain Chieftain Lygari's admiration.

He took down the tent without even being asked, rolled the cow hides round the poles and helped to rope them onto Haski. Then he spotted the leather pouch containing the King's Table set, still lying on the boulder where they had sat to play the night before.

Lucky I noticed, or we would have left it behind, he thought. *Should I point it out to him? No, he might think I'm criticising him for being careless. I'll just quietly put it away in his saddlebag.*

But Lygari was already busy with his bag, rummaging around in it.

Better not disturb him. I'll look after it myself until we stop again. Then I can sneak it into his bag while he's doing something else.

So he stowed the gaming set in his own saddlebag, taking great care to keep it away from his food. Then he swung himself up onto Elf's saddle – surprised at how nimbly he could do this now – and was ready to set off even before the chieftain.

They rode steadily through the colourless desert towards the mountains, then climbed up a steep pass. Here the wind came screaming at them, whipping up their cloaks and the horses' manes. But as usual, Magnus found the jingling horse rattles calmed his nervousness, though they also made him feel rather drowsy. He managed to stay awake long enough to see the stunning views from the top of the pass – right across the desert and Salmon Valley – then nodded off.

By the time he forced his eyes open again, they were coming down towards some low, orange-brown hills, topped by billowing columns of smoke.

32

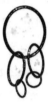

The Fiery Holes formed an abominable monstrosity in the heart of the desert. It lay off a lonely road between Salmon Valley and the distant farms of the east coast, used by only the most intrepid travellers. The ground around it was said to be treacherous: blistering hot, constantly shifting and crumbling. All the children had been strongly forbidden ever to go anywhere near it.

'Exactly the sort of place Grim Gruesome would take his victims to be tortured!' said Asny. 'Good thinking, Kari.'

'Let's go there, then – now!' begged Sigrid. She jumped up.

But Asny shook her head. 'Don't be stupid. It's a really long way into the desert. We need to pack food – for the horses as well as for us – or we'll never make it there. We need time to get ready.'

'Ya, and if you don't want anyone to spot what we're up to, the best time to leave is the middle of the night,' said Ref.

Reluctantly, Sigrid agreed to ride back to Underhill Farm. They would all go to bed as normal, and when everyone else was fast asleep, they would creep out secretly and meet again at the ford.

It was well past midnight and the summer dawn was already breaking. The four children's horses splashed across the river, each laden with a bag full of food and a bundle of hay.

Ref led the way on his brown-and-white horse, Warrior. He was closely tailed by Asny and Kari on their light-brown horses, Swift-Foot and Mischief. Sigrid and Faithful followed a remorseful distance behind.

On the far side of the ford, they set out along a rough track. This soon swung round into the flat desert wastelands and became increasingly difficult to follow, for years of bad weather had blown away its markings. However, a series of large, upright boulders had been set up here and there to show the way.

The terrain was all stone and rock: flat, colourless and dry. Above them, the sun wove in and out of wind-streaked clouds. The indistinct road led towards a distant cluster of barren, orange-brown hills.

All through the morning, the horses plodded on calmly, uncomplaining, never stopping unless they spotted a dribbling stream or spring where they could drink. The children hardly spoke at all.

At last they drew close enough to see that the hills ahead were made entirely of sand. The marker stones showed the road passing right round them. However Ref stopped and pointed up one of the slopes.

'See it?' he called. 'Smell it? We need to turn off here.'

White steam was drifting over the hilltop, bringing a strong stink of bad eggs.

The horses began to climb the slope, slowly and reluctantly.

At the top the children dismounted, and gave the horses their hay. They peered down to see an extraordinary, dream-like landscape spread before them.

Orange-brown sand covered the whole area. It was coated with weird crusts of something thick and white, and littered with misshapen rocks. In-between were many curiously shaped craters, each one full of something blue-grey.

The bad eggs smell was almost suffocating.

There was steam everywhere. It rose from the craters. It hung over small, evil-looking streams that trickled through cracks in the arid hillsides. It hissed out of fumaroles – weird, cone-shaped mounds of red-hot rock and ash.

Suddenly Kari nudged them all and pointed. 'Look – there are people down there – and horses!'

'Get back behind the ridge before they see us,' hissed Ref.

Hurriedly, they stumbled back a few paces and dropped to the ground. Lying on their stomachs, they wriggled back up the sandy slope, so they could peer over the ridge without being seen.

33

Magnus had a huge grin on his face as he slipped off Elf's back and followed Chieftain Lygari round the Fiery Holes. He couldn't stop chattering.

'Do you know, sir,' he said, 'I've always wanted to see this place, and it's even better than I imagined. What amazing colours! And look over there, sir! That's not water in there – like you said, it's boiling *mud!*'

He pointed towards a steaming crater with sheer grey sides and a cracked, white rim. The liquid in it was a vivid blue-grey. It bubbled, rippled and gurgled – *Blurp! Slop! Thleeeeh!* – sending up spurting fountains of sludge.

Chieftain Lygari strode across to it, Magnus trailing after him.

'Perhaps you have forgotten why I brought you here, Magnus?' the chieftain growled. 'It's not to gawp at the scenery, is it?'

Magnus tittered nervously.

The chieftain stopped dead, grabbed Magnus by the shoulders and shook him hard. 'Are you daring to mock me, you worthless maggot?'

'No, sir, of course not,' said Magnus quickly. 'Um, we're here so I can carry out my forfeit.'

'And what is your forfeit?'

'I've…er…I've got to, you know, jump into one of those mud-pools,' said Magnus. He suddenly realised that they were horribly close to the edge of the crater. He tried to move away, but the chieftain's grip was like an iron clamp.

'And?'

'And… Er, I can't actually remember you saying anything else,' said Magnus. 'Well, I think you said that the mud-pool would cook me, but obviously you were joking…'

'I was not, Magnus,' said the chieftain. He pointed at the crater with his throbbing finger-stump. 'This is for real. I am ordering you: GET INTO THAT MUD-POOL!'

Farting, flea-bitten giantesses with big white wobbling bottoms! thought Magnus. *I reckon he really means it!*

A cold shudder ran through him.

But...but WHY? I thought I'd impressed him. What did I do wrong?

Worms seemed to be wriggling through his stomach.

Ma, Pa – save me!

His legs felt as if they were dissolving into butter.

What am I going to do?

He still felt muzzy from the ride and the constant jingling of the rattles: his thoughts wouldn't come together.

'I...I'm sorry, sir,' he stammered. 'I don't understand. Wh...why do I have to do this? Well, I know it's because I lost those games... Oh! Is it also because you're angry that I *beat* you at King's Table that other time we played? I never thought you'd mind, I swear I didn't mean to offend you... *Have* I offended you, sir?'

Chieftain Lygari was grasping him so tightly that Magnus feared his bones would be crushed to splinters. 'Of course you have offended me. *All* children offend me!'

Magnus stared at him in bewilderment.

Play for time, he thought. His mind cleared and began to race. *I know! I could just PRETEND to do what he wants...*

He gazed desperately around and spotted a mud-pool nearby that looked both shallow and barely hot enough to be steaming. He pointed at it, trying to wriggle free of the chieftain's grip.

'I'll jump in here, sir,' he cried. 'See, I'm doing what you've ordered: I'm carrying out the forfeit straightaway.'

'Not in that pathetic sucklings' paddling pool!' the chieftain roared. 'In this new game, Magnus, *I* make all the rules. *I* decide where and how you will pay your forfeit.'

'But that's not fair!' cried Magnus.

The chieftain dragged Magnus across the rock-strewn sand, towards one of the fumarole mounds. It was a gigantic heap of smouldering ashes and lumps of molten, red-brown rock. Steam hissed loudly from it, like an overheated cauldron.

Magnus struggled. He could see Elf and Haski standing some way off, with the desert spread behind them.

FFZZZ! The stinking billow of steam engulfed them. The landscape vanished and the world turned white. Magnus choked…

ZZZSHHH! They emerged suddenly back into the

fresh air, right by the brink of another pool. *SLURP! LOBLOBALOB! SISSH!* Its blue-grey mud bubbled and spouted as if a fierce monster was writhing below the surface, or an underwater volcano was starting to explode. Burning heat rose from the ground: Magnus could feel it dissolving the leather soles of his shoes. Sweat trickled down his body.

'JUMP IN THERE!' Chieftain Lygari roared at him.

'But sir, if I do that – I'll die!' cried Magnus.

'Of course you will die, you loser,' snapped Chieftain Lygari. 'And your crabby little boy's flesh will be cooked in the molten earth-fires until it is completely tender. Then I shall tear it off your bones and gobble you up!'

Magnus teetered on the edge of the pool. *I can't!* he thought. *Ma, save me!*

'MAGNUS!'

Suddenly a loud shout tore through the air. Chieftain Lygari loosened his grip and spun round.

Magnus managed to turn too – and almost fainted with astonishment. For there were Kari, Ref and Asny, running down from the ridge, and heading straight towards them!

34

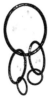

'Get away from him!' yelled Kari. 'He's no chieftain – he's a fraud. He's that child killer – Grim Gruesome!'

Magnus's mouth dropped open.

Grim Gruesome gave a bellow of laughter that bounced and echoed all around the wilderness. He let go of Magnus and strode towards the other children.

Magnus quickly stepped back from the mud-pool. *The evil, cunning brute!* he thought. *But what a brilliant trick! Fancy actually warning us that Grim Gruesome was in Iceland when it was really HIM all along! That horrible finger-stump…keeping his face hidden… Aw! and his name even means "liar"! Why didn't I see through it?*

He felt winded, as if someone had rammed a block of ice into his bowels. Memories flashed through his mind's eye: the so-called 'chieftain' making himself at home in their farmhouse, hoodwinking the whole family with his self importance; the feel of his heavily scarred skin when they shook hands.

He even fooled Ma and Pa! he thought. *Pa said they were friends! Ma let him sleep on our bench by our fire…*

Suddenly he felt really sick.

And – flaming sheep poo! – last night I slept next to him in his tent. He could have killed me there and then!

Through the billowing steam, he saw the other three children at the foot of the slope, running across the sand; and Grim Gruesome taking gigantic, demented steps towards them.

He heard Ref shouting: 'Magnus, the Rings of Doom – they're the rattle – on that horse you've been riding!'

But those rings that were left to Sigrid? Magnus thought. *Of course! Another trick, to fool us we were safe!*

Shock and horror rushed through him, followed by the blinding darkness of rage, until his whole body was bristling.

He put his head down – raced after Grim Gruesome – and charged him like a mad bull.

'You beast!' he shrieked. 'You liar! You fraud! I hate you!'

His head collided with something stone-hard –

Grim Gruesome's backside? He thumped it fiercely – but only managed to hurt his own hand. A gust of wind flapped the villain's voluminous, stinking cloak into Magnus's face. Untangling himself, he heard a piercing whistle – then the drumming of hooves.

Haski galloped up, closely followed by Elf. Grim Gruesome seized Magnus and hurled him onto Elf's back. Magnus clutched her mane and struggled to get off... But the jingling rattles overwhelmed him. *The Rings of Doom at work,* he thought vaguely. *Making me dozy...in Grim Gruesome's power... Farting giantesses! Look what he's doing to the horses!*

Grim Gruesome was moving his finger-stump at them in an undulating circle, scattering yellow drips of pus. They began to buck and rear: UP AND DOWN, UP – UP – CRASH DOWN... Magnus clung to Elf for dear life. They bounded round the pools in a rush of sand, steam and rippling mud... UP AGAIN!

Magnus tried to grab the reins but failed. He slid down Elf's back – screamed as he saw the bubbling crater just behind him – then at the last moment threw himself forward and wrapped his arms tightly round her neck. Her creamy mane blew into his mouth. He spat it out and clung on, trembling violently.

35

Sigrid was literally frozen with terror. She didn't run down to the Fiery Holes with the other three children. She didn't even peer over the ridge to watch them. Instead she squatted beside the grazing horses, biting her nails and snivelling.

'Sigrid!' Asny came racing back. 'It *is* Grim Gruesome down there!' She spat out the news in short, breathless gasps. 'He's forcing Magnus into the boiling mud. Elf is all spooked, she's bucking and rearing…!'

Sigrid groaned.

'Stop blabbering and get up!' snapped Asny. She slapped Sigrid's face. 'You're the only one who can calm a horse in that state – you've got to come!'

She hauled Sigrid to her feet, pushed her across to Faithful and into the saddle, then steered the horse round to the ridge, nagging and scolding mercilessly until Sigrid began to ride down the slope.

At the bottom, Faithful carried Sigrid round a wafting cloud of steam. Then he suddenly stopped and swished his tail – for Ref and Kari were standing a short way off, white-faced and trembling...and just beyond them was Grim Gruesome!

The brute seemed to have grown enormous. His cloak billowed monstrously in the wind and he was brandishing two heavily blood-stained swords. Sigrid's heart turned over. She tugged at the reins – but Grim Gruesome had already seen her.

'Come and share the fun, while I beat up these two maggots, Sigrid,' he roared. 'Help me whet my appetite before I cook Magnus and gobble him up – and make your great wish come true!'

He hurled one of the swords at Ref, lunging at him with the other one. Sigrid screamed. Faithful snorted and galloped on.

They heard the ominous sound of horse-rattles. Then they passed through more steam and emerged in an area with bubbling mud-pools on every side. And there was Magnus! He was clinging precariously to Elf's back, shrieking with terror as the white horse sprang around crazily after the great black stallion, Haski.

Kringle, kringle! Kringle, kringle!

UP – CRASH DOWN – UP AGAIN!

The Rings of Doom were a numbing razzle-dazzle of sound. Sigrid gritted her teeth, struggling with all her might to resist it. Half-dreams and memories spurted randomly through her mind.

What did Chieftain Lygari – Grim Gruesome! – say when he gave me Elf? Ya, that's it: 'Whatever you do, don't take the rattle off her.'

A shiver ran down her spine.

Well, he's told me himself that he's a liar. So, if I'm going to save Magnus, I need to do the OPPOSITE of what he says – I need to cut Elf's rattle off her bridle. But how?

Suddenly it came to her: *That gift from the weird women!* She reached under her cloak to the trinkets dangling from her shoulder-brooch and yanked off the metal file.

Scarcely daring to breathe, she guided Faithful back to the other two horses, dodging Haski's flailing hooves. She drew alongside Magnus and Elf. Clutching the file in one hand, she leaned over and strained towards Elf's bridle.

But before she could reach it, Haski leaped between them:

'NE-E-HE-ECCHHH!'

He turned and arched his towering neck across Faithful's head, clamping them both against him.

Sigrid whimpered in despair. But Faithful twisted up, bared his teeth bravely and bit at Haski's throat. Haski squealed and lurched away. Faithful spun round and dived right underneath the great stallion, Sigrid ducking just in time. They came out safely on the other side and ran at Haski again. Faithful twisted, kicked and nipped, over and over – until, unbelievably, Haski began to back away.

Meanwhile, Elf was still jittering madly about, trying to toss Magnus into the deadly mud. *Kringle, kringle! Kringle, kringle!* The rattles were almost deafening. Sigrid steered Faithful level with Elf again, stretched across… And this time actually managed to grab the metal clip that linked Elf's bridle to the Rings of Doom.

Frantically, she rubbed at the clip with the file. Elf's ears flicked fitfully. Magnus shrieked. The file went back-and-forth, back-and-forth…

Suddenly the clip gave way. The Rings of Doom came free and fell to the ground with a loud *KSSHH!*

Elf skidded to a halt. Magnus finally lost his grip

and tumbled sideways. He bumped against the saddlebag and crashed after it onto the hot sand, landing awkwardly on his knees, right next to the broken Rings.

'You...you *saved* me, Sigrid!' he managed to say incredulously. 'Th...thank you!'

Then he keeled over.

36

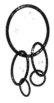

Grim Gruesome had forced Ref and Kari to fight him, taking turns to wield the sword he had hurled at them. Though they were two against one, and Asny had run back to yell encouragement, the fight was *not* going well. The sword was so heavy that neither boy could swing it properly, and they were both badly bruised and bloodied.

However, every so often Grim Gruesome turned round to check what was happening to Magnus. When he saw Haski pawing the ground by the boy's slumped body, and Elf standing motionless nearby, he ceased his battering, snatched back his spare sword, kicked Ref and Kari to the ground, then marched over.

He nudged Magnus with his toe, and bellowed with triumph when he didn't move. Next, he strode across to Sigrid and dragged her roughly out of Faithful's saddle.

173

'Look, your poor little brother's died of fright, Sigrid,' he jeered, pointing at Magnus with his finger-stump. 'I've made your great wish come true!'

Sigrid let out a loud sob. But Faithful backed into Grim Gruesome, kicking up his hind hooves at the villain's belly. With a furious roar, Grim Gruesome aimed his great, whale hide boot at Faithful's flank.

'Don't hurt him!' screamed Sigrid.

But Faithful was already bolting up the hill.

Despite Grim Gruesome's gloating, Magnus was actually very much alive. He wasn't even badly stunned. He soon came back to his senses and at once his mind started buzzing.

Pretend to be dead! he thought. *That'll fool the brute...give me valuable time.*

He had fallen awkwardly on top of his saddlebag. As the buckle dug painfully into his chest, an idea flashed into his head.

The King's Table board! he thought. *It's still inside my bag. It's so shiny, if someone stood on it, they'd slide about all over the place. And those spikes on the playing pieces are really sharp...*

He lay absolutely still, mulling this over, peering furtively around. Surreptitiously, he shifted his weight off the saddlebag. He grasped the buckle and fiddled it loose, then carefully opened the flap. He thrust his hand inside, past the remains of his picnic, to the soft leather pouch containing the gaming set. He drew it out, then stood up.

Unfortunately, at exactly the same moment, Grim Gruesome turned round.

He hurled Sigrid to the ground and set Haski to stand guard over her, hooves astride her shoulders. Then he advanced upon Magnus, brandishing his sword.

Magnus whipped the gaming board from its pouch and thrust a clutch of playing pieces into its holes.

Grim Gruesome was almost upon him!

Magnus darted away, clutching the board, heading for a sizzling, steaming fumarole.

37

Sand spattered around Faithful's hooves as he galloped up the orange-brown hill, his head exploding with horrible thoughts.

FEAR. PAIN. FLEE!

At the top he found Warrior, Swift-Foot and Mischief still munching at their food placidly. They whinnied him a greeting. He stood very still until he gradually calmed down. Then he went to slurp up some hay.

But he couldn't chew it.

SIGRID.

Her face was vivid in his mind's eye. He remembered the warmth of her hand, gentle on his nose, her voice calling his name.

HAPPINESS.

They had shared their lives ever since he was a

lanky foal, had grown together into mature horse and skillful rider.

He dropped the hay. The wind moaned over the hill-top, bringing the scent of Sigrid's distress.

Faithful lifted his head high and pricked his ears.

SIGRID. DANGER!

The other horses all stopped eating and turned to watch him, poised to run.

38

Sigrid was totally trapped by Haski, lying face down between his gigantic black legs. She tried not to cry, tried not to imagine what Grim Gruesome was doing to Magnus.

'NE-EE-EH-EHH!'

Suddenly a loud chorus of whinnies rang across the wilderness. Haski's legs tensed. Cautiously, Sigrid lifted her head and gazed around at the steam, sand and mud-pools, and the orange-brown hills behind. Right at the top of these, four horses stood silhouetted against the sky, then came galloping down the slope.

Goddess Freyja's amber tears! thought Sigrid. *That's my Faithful leading the others! Whatever are they doing?*

The horses raced right down to the Fiery Holes. They stampeded past Magnus and Grim Gruesome. Their hooves thundered on the warm sand. Soon they drew level with Elf. She stirred and a ripple ran through her creamy mane. It was as if she was waking after a long sleep. Her ears darted from side to side and her nostrils quivered. She stamped her front hoof three times. Then suddenly she sprang to life and leaped after the others.

So now there were five horses, galloping straight at Sigrid and Haski. How small they were compared to Haski! Yet how boldly they closed in on him!

Sigrid curled into a ball to protect herself, shielding her face with her hands. She heard the horses pounding around her, glimpsed a suffocating blur of legs and swirling tails...

Then everything fell still.

Warm breath blew at her neck. Sigrid uncurled herself, dropped her hands and gazed up into Faithful's dark eye. Behind him stood Warrior, Swift-Foot, Mischief – and Elf.

Sigrid struggled to her feet. In the distance, she saw Haski galloping away in a cloud of dust, disappearing towards the wastes of the desert. Sigrid took a few shaky steps, and almost tripped over a tangle of metal. It was the two horse-rattles – the Rings of Doom – all trampled and broken. Gingerly, she picked them up.

39

Magnus had almost reached the fumarole. It looked like a miniature volcano, no higher than he was, its sides formed from sand, white crusts and black ash. Its summit was piled with red-hot rocks, vibrating and tumbling to the ground as steam hissed up beneath them.

Grim Gruesome was getting closer. And closer.

Magnus ducked into the steam cloud and rushed right round the fumarole, almost back to where he had started. However, now he was *behind* Grim Gruesome.

He took a deep breath. Then he hurled the gaming board with all his might.

The board arced through the air. Bubbles of steam glistened on its deeply polished surface.

It fell, skidded across the sand, hit a rock and bounced back. The playing pieces shot from the holes and scattered to the ground, their sharp spikes sticking upwards.

Grim Gruesome heard the noise behind him and spun round. As the villain lunged out to seize Magnus, his left foot landed on top of the slippery board. The board wobbled. Grim Gruesome's boot slithered. His right foot smashed down on top of several spikes and twisted awkwardly. The board slid away in the opposite direction, taking his left foot with it. He teetered, cursing and swearing.

At that very moment, the five horses reached the fumarole. As one, they plunged through the steam – and charged.

A bone-chilling roar echoed across the Fiery Holes.

The children, scattered around the evil landscape, all froze.

Then Sigrid came came running from one direction, Asny from the other, with Ref and Kari limping bravely behind her.

'Thor's thunderbolts!' cried Kari. He elbowed Magnus. 'Look at *that*!'

As the steam thinned away, it revealed the horses all

gathered around Grim Gruesome. The villain had pitched right across the fumarole. He was bellowing like a wounded bull. For a heart-stopping moment it seemed that he would scrabble off, leap free and hurl one of the children onto the deadly pyre in his place...

But his monstrous strength was useless against the scorching rocks and belching steam. As he jerked about, trying to kick himself free, struggling and roaring, the fumarole crumbled under his weight. It caved inwards and began to suck him down, like ravenous quicksand.

'Flaming sheep poo!' breathed Magnus.

The villain was actually disappearing before their eyes! The children stared and stared, squealing with shock and disbelief.

Sigrid was the first to wrench herself away, distracted by the two broken rattles still dangling from her fingers.

'I ought to get rid of these,' she said. She hesitated, then nudged Magnus. 'Um...do you want to help me?'

Magnus didn't answer.

Sigrid shrugged.

She walked slowly across to a large mud-pool. As she stood on the rim, preparing to throw the rattles in, she realised that Magnus had come up behind her.

'You can do it, if you want,' she offered awkwardly.

'Why don't we take one each?' said Magnus. 'Then we can chuck them away together.'

And so they did.

Kringle, kringle!

The rings dazzled briefly, black iron and gleaming silver, sharp against the desert light. Then the blue-grey mud plopped, surged up – and swallowed them.

The next moment, there was a thunderous roar behind them. The fumarole was erupting! They dashed back...

But by the time they arrived, there was nothing left of it. The mound of rocks and ashes had exploded itself to nothing. Its steam-hole was filled with dust. And Grim Gruesome had completely vanished into its noxious depths.

'He's finished!' yelled Kari.

'Destroyed!' shouted Magnus.

Asny looked at Sigrid, then held out her hand. Sigrid gulped...then took it.

The next moment, the two girls were hugging and sobbing on each other's shoulders.

Ref let out a hearty sigh of relief.

40

'The Rings of Doom are no more!'

'Grim Gruesome is destroyed!'

'Iceland is saved by five brave children!'

The first winter snow was fluttering down. Groa, Helga and Vigdis had been walking for months, leaving Salmon Valley far behind and wearing out countless shoes. Now they were waddling through the green valleys above Iceland's east coast. Every time they passed a farm, they shouted the news at the tops of their voices, and people came running across the frozen fields to find out more.

'Grim Gruesome? We had no idea that evil brute was in Iceland!'

'How did these children destroy him?'

'Who are they? Have they been rewarded?'

The weird women waggled their gnarled fingers

and shook their heads mysteriously.

'It was Grim Gruesome who brought the Rings of Doom, lady – but nobody knows how or when,' said Vigdis.

'They destroyed him by cunning, fire and a herd of fighting horses,' said Groa.

'They're the bravest children in Iceland,' said Helga importantly. 'And we've met two of them, the brother and sister, Magnus and Sigrid. We've been inside their house!'

'We reported their deeds to the Great Thing,' said Groa. 'And their parents formally complained that the chieftains should have warned them that such a false and dangerous villain was on the loose.'

'So the chieftains awarded the children a great hoard of treasure!' said Helga. 'Some was compensation for failing to protect them; but it was mostly a reward for their astonishing bravery.'

'Ya,' said Vigdis disapprovingly. 'That Magnus got so many silver bars, it took two days to dig a hole in the ground big enough to hide them all. And Sigrid got a pure white bearskin for her saddle, and more jewellery than the Queen of Norway! They're totally spoiled.'

'No they're not,' said Helga. 'They're both too busy for that. You see, Magnus is learning to recite the laws: he's so talented, he might become Law Speaker one day. As for Sigrid, she rescued her brother's horse, Elf, from the villain. And her own horse, Faithful, actually overpowered Grim Gruesome! People are so impressed, that they're paying her to train *their* horses too.'

'Most people who hear our news, throw a feast to celebrate the destruction of Grim Gruesome,' said Groa pointedly.

Of course, every farmwife who heard this felt obliged to keep up with the others, and organise a feast herself. So Groa, Vigdis and Helga did very well out of the five children's extraordinary adventure. By the time winter was over, all three were fatter than they had ever been in their lives!

However, unfortunately their news was not totally true. For although Sigrid, Magnus, Ref, Asny, and Kari believed that Grim Gruesome had vanished for ever into the fiery bowels of the earth, they were wrong. It seems that somehow he survived and managed to climb out from the debris of the fumarole; and that Haski emerged from the desert to find him.

For when the autumn nights drew in, several travellers saw a gigantic, cloaked figure on a long-legged horse galloping over the mountain ridges. Later, other people saw him on the shore below the forbidding wastes of the Water Glacier, then rowing out into the iceberg-riddled sea.

These people claimed that, as well as his rotten finger-stump, his burned arms, his black spittle and one eyeball hanging on a thread from its socket, now the villain also had one foot twisted back-to-front from his fall on the spikes and the gaming board. They said that this deepened his hatred of all children.

No doubt you'd love to know what he did to take his revenge. But you'll have to wait, for that's another very grim and gruesome story!

'Wolf-guts! Whale-doom! This I swear:
I'll stalk vile children everywhere.
I'll snatch and spike them in my snare
and boil their bones in dark despair!'

Iceland is a wild and very beautiful country full of volcanoes and hot springs. While this book was being written, it suffered a major volcanic eruption at Eyjafjallajökull, which sent a huge cloud of ash all over Europe. A second eruption took place just as the story was finished – this time from a volcano called Grimsvötn (which means Grim's Water!).

Most Viking countries were kingdoms, but the Icelanders didn't believe in kings. Instead they were ruled by a group of all-male chieftains, who met regularly at open-air public meetings called *things*. The *Althing* (Great Thing) was for the whole country and was held once a year in June.

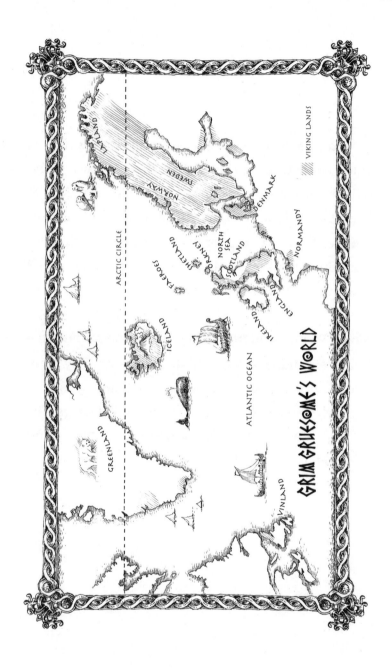

GRIM GRUESOME'S WORLD

LAPLAND
SWEDEN
NORWAY
DENMARK
VIKING LANDS
NORMANDY
NORTH SEA
ORKNEY
SCOTLAND
SHETLAND
ENGLAND
FAEROES
IRELAND
ARCTIC CIRCLE
ICELAND
ATLANTIC OCEAN
GREENLAND
VINLAND

GRIM GRUESOME
VIKING VILLAIN

THE CURSED SWORD

Experience a pirate ship, a mighty sword and a fortune teller... Read the runes carved into an evil curse... travel to the frozen north... And climb a mountain to Grim Gruesome's forest lair!

THE QUEEN'S POISON

Meet a fearsome berserk warrior and a queen who's supposed to be a witch... Shudder at threats of shape-changing... And get swept away on horseback by the evil Grim Gruesome!

TROLLS' TREASURE

Quest to find a wonderful treasure... Survive in the wilds as an outlaw... Get locked inside a dark mound haunted by trolls... And have another narrow escape from the evil Grim Gruesome!

Have you visited
the Grim Gruesome website yet?

go to:

www.grimgruesome.com

★ Find out more about the Grim Gruesome books

★ Discover lots of interesting facts about the
   Viking Age

★ Do the Grim Gruesome quiz and puzzles

★ Learn to play the Viking game of King's Table -
   like Magnus and Grim Gruesome

★ Meet author Rosalind Kerven